Quietly, Ma
Walked in.
bed. 'Kels?'
'It's OK. Just a bad d

'I couldn't save them, Matt. I *failed*.'

'It wasn't your fault. Nobody expected the fire to suddenly come shooting out like that. None of the rest of the crew could have done more,' he reminded her. 'And look at today. You made a difference today. If it wasn't for you, Noel could have been in a really bad way. You got him out while we could still help him.'

'It's still not enough.'

'Hey.' He shifted to pull the duvet aside and slid into the bed beside her. 'Come here.' He pulled her into his arms, pillowing her head against his chest. She was shaking. Still crying? He wasn't sure, though her face was damp. He held her close, stroking her hair and soothing her. 'It's going to be all right, Kels. I promise,' he whispered. She'd be safe in his arms. Always.

And eventually she stopped shaking. Curled her arms round him. 'Thanks, Matt. For being here. For—well. You know.'

'Any time.' He dropped a kiss on her hair.

Kate Hardy lives on the outskirts of Norwich with her husband, two small children, two lazy spaniels—and too many books to count! She wrote her first book at age six, when her parents gave her a typewriter for her birthday. She had the first of a series of sexy romances published at twenty-five, and swapped a job in marketing communications for freelance health journalism when her son was born, so she could spend more time with him. She's wanted to write for Mills & Boon since she was twelve—and when she was pregnant with her daughter, her husband pointed out that writing Medical Romances™ would be the perfect way to combine her interest in health issues with her love of good stories. It really is the best of both worlds—especially as she gets to meet a new gorgeous hero every time...Kate is always delighted to hear from readers—do drop in to her website at www.katehardy.com

Recent books by Kate Hardy:

THE CONSULTANT'S CHRISTMAS PROPOSAL
HER CELEBRITY SURGEON
   (*Posh Docs* trilogy Book 1)
HER HONOURABLE PLAYBOY
   (*Posh Docs* trilogy Book 2)
HIS HONOURABLE SURGEON
   (*Posh Docs* trilogy Book 3)

THE FIREFIGHTER'S FIANCÉ

BY
KATE HARDY

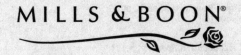

First published in Great Britain 2006
Harlequin Mills & Boon Limited,
Eton House, 18-24 Paradise Road, Richmond, Surrey TW9 1SR

© Pamela Brooks 2006

Standard ISBN 0 263 84747 0
Promotional ISBN 0 263 85136 2

Set in Times Roman 10½ on 12 pt
03-0806-49816

Printed and bound in Spain
by Litografia Rosés, S.A., Barcelona

THE
FIREFIGHTER'S
FIANCÉ

For the Blue Watch at Bethel Street,
with many thanks for the tour and the talk!

CHAPTER ONE

THE familiar warble burst into the air, then the Tannoy announced, 'Turnout, vehicle 57. RTC. Lorry and car, driver trapped.'

RTC. Three little letters that had blown Kelsey's life apart. Changed it completely. Had it not happened, she'd have been a maths teacher by now. Married, maybe with a child.

But it *had* happened.

Five years ago. The driver of the car on the other side of the road had been concentrating on his mobile phone instead of the road and had hit their car head on. Kelsey had walked away without even a scratch, whereas her fiancé Danny had been rushed to hospital, with surgeons tutting at the foot of his bed and saying he'd be lucky to make it. She'd sat by his bedside for days, not sure if he'd ever come to.

And then he'd squeezed her hand.

She'd cried with relief, sure that everything was going to be OK and it was the beginning of the long road back to normal… But the day the doctors had told Danny he'd never walk again and he'd spend the rest of his life in a wheelchair, he'd asked Kelsey to return his ring. Hadn't accepted that the wheelchair made no difference, in her eyes. 'I don't know what I want any more, Kelsey. I don't know who I *am* any more.'

She knew who he was. The love of her life. The man she wanted to support back to health. The man she *should* nurse back to health.

But he didn't let her. She wasn't enough for him. 'I care about you, Kelsey. I always will. But I don't want to get married to you any more. I need…' He shook his head. 'I don't know what I need.'

Whatever, it wasn't *her*. And Danny pushed her out of his life. Nothing she said or did was able to change his mind. Their parents, their friends: nobody was able to get through to him. It was over and he wanted her to walk away.

And in the end she had to accept it. Accept that she wasn't what he wanted any more. That he needed to adjust to his new life, and she wasn't going to be part of it.

She wasn't able to face carrying out the rest of their plans on her own. The life they'd intended. So she sold their house, split the proceeds with Danny. And she walked out of her teacher training course. Being a maths teacher would have reminded her too much of the life they'd planned together. So she applied to train for something completely different. Something that would make a difference.

She became a firefighter.

A good one.

Payback, in her eyes, for having her own life saved.

Every time she heard the call over the Tannoy saying it was an RTC, it still sent adrenalin coursing through her veins. Brought back the memories, the shaky feeling, the fear that she wouldn't get out alive. But every time she shoved the emotions back where they belonged. In the past. Because she had a job to do.

The same job she needed to do right now.

Kelsey was the nearest to the fax machine, so she ripped off the top copy and headed straight for her fire engine. The rest of the crew were sliding down the pole from the mess room and getting into their firefighting gear, which was set out ready by the doors of the fire engine—the jackets hung up, the boots ready to be stepped into and the trousers neatly rolled down round them, so they didn't have to waste time getting things in the right order. It was a routine she knew well—one she'd practised in drill after drill, and done plenty of times before real emergency calls. She kicked off her shoes and stepped into her boots, pulled her trousers up, shrugged on her jacket and climbed into her place in the rear of the engine.

Ray, the station manager, was already in the front seat, tapping into the computer. Kelsey handed him the fax and he scanned it, taking in the map reference and details. 'Another driver's called us, the police and the ambulance. Nothing about any other casualties or what sort of state the road's in. Better put your PPE and conspicuity surcoats on now,' he said to the crew. Joe, being the driver, was exempt until they'd stopped—then he'd need to put on the gear before he got out onto the carriageway.

'What's the plan, guv?' Kelsey asked.

'If the police get there first, they can set up traffic diversion. If we're there first, we need the "police accident" sign up while I do the risk assessment,' Ray said. 'Kelsey, you're the one with ALS training.'

As well as doing an advanced life support course, she shared a house with Matt, a paramedic, which meant she'd picked up a fair bit about casualty management.

'If the ambo team aren't there, I'll need you to check out the casualties,' Ray added.

'Sure, guv.' Kelsey nodded.

'Road conditions good,' Ray reported back to Control. 'Visibility fine.'

It wasn't ice or fog or heavy rain that had caused the crash. It was a summer afternoon, and the sun wasn't yet low enough to dazzle a driver. So Kelsey's best guess would be speed. That, or someone deciding to ignore the law and use a mobile phone without a hands-free kit—and then discovering the hard way that you couldn't use a phone and drive safely at the same time.

Something she already knew, from extremely bitter experience.

She pushed the thoughts aside and concentrated on her job.

It turned out that the fire crew were the first on the scene. Joe parked on the side in front of the crashed lorry; Ray, as the officer in charge, did the risk assessment and radioed back to Base. 'Dual carriageway, bit of a tailback but access is fine on the main road. Other carriageway fine, just the usual rubber-necking. No injured casualties on the carriageway. We're going to check the vehicles now. No hazardous materials being carried that we know of. Some fuel spillage that needs containing.'

Ray directed his crew to contain and absorb the fuel spillage, and lay out the firefighting equipment to cover the area. 'Brains, can you check the casualties and report back?'

'Sure, guv.' Kelsey smiled back at him, not minding the nickname. The crew had chosen it once they'd found out what she'd done before she'd become a firefighter—and it told her that she was accepted. Part of the team.

The lorry driver was shaking, clearly in shock, and Kelsey took the space blanket from their limited medical kit and put it round his shoulders. 'OK, love. The ambulance will be here soon. Any pain I need to tell the medics about when they get here?'

'No, I'm all right. But, oh, God. The other driver…' He shuddered. 'I can still feel his car going under my wheels.'

'What happened?' she asked gently.

The lorry driver shook his head. 'The road's clear. I dunno. I was doing sixty. Everything was fine. He must have been going past me, in my blind spot—next thing I knew, he was…' The driver choked.

Kelsey glanced at the carriageway. From the pattern of skidmarks and the dent in the central reservation, it looked as if the driver had hit the barrier, spun round and ricocheted back into the path of the lorry.

'OK, love. Come and sit down at the side of the road. Take a deep breath for me. And another. That's right.' She guided him to a safe waiting place. 'The medics'll be here any minute now. I'm just going to take a look at the car and see what I can do for the driver, OK? But someone will be here to see you very, very soon. If you need anything, come and see one of us, but make sure you stay on the hard shoulder, where it's safe.'

'My wife. I ought to…' He swallowed hard.

Kelsey guessed what he was trying to say. 'We'll get in contact with her for you, love. Soon as the police are here. Don't use your radio or mobile phone here, will you? Fire risk,' she said economically. There was a ten-metre exclusion zone from the incident for using radios or mobile phones—a spark could ignite any leaking fuel. She patted his shoulder. 'Back with you in a bit, OK?'

She steeled herself for a closer look at the car. No way was the driver going to get out of the car and walk away without a scratch. But at least there wasn't a bull's-eye on the windscreen, so either his airbag had kicked in or he'd just been lucky and hadn't hit the windscreen head first.

There wasn't a huge amount she could do before the ambulance arrived. But she could go through the basics—the course she'd taken plus what she'd learned from Matt would help.

ABCDE, she reminded herself. Work through it. The same way Matt did. Airway, breathing, circulation, disability, exposure.

She could see that the driver's door was jammed but tried it anyway. No luck. Same with the passenger's side. But she could at least get into the back—once the car was stabilised. From the damage to the car, she thought there was a high risk of the driver having some sort of cervical spine injury, so they needed to make sure the car didn't move.

She opened the rear door on the driver's side so she could at least talk to him. 'I'm Kelsey, one of the fire crew,' she said. 'The ambulance is on its way. What's your name, love?'

'Harvey.'

Good. He could speak. So his airway was clear, not blocked with blood or vomit. His breathing seemed a bit shallow; she couldn't get a proper look to see if he was losing any blood or had circulation problems; but he'd managed to answer a question and sounded lucid, so that ticked off 'disability' because there weren't any immediate neurological problems. Exposure, so they could see the extent of his injuries…Well, that would have to wait until they'd cut him out. Even an experienced paramedic like Matt would find it tough to get the driver out of this space, so the odds were they'd have to use the hydraulic equipment—known as a Hurst, but they'd all been told to use the longer name because in the muffled environment of a crash vehicle the short name sounded more like 'hearse' and terrified the casualties.

'Can you tell me if you've got any pain?' she asked.

'My neck,' he said.

Could be whiplash; could be a spinal injury. She made a mental note to tell the paramedics. 'As soon as the ambulance is here, we'll get a collar on you and get you out.'

'My legs. Hurt.'

Well, that was good. It was when they *didn't* feel pain that she was worried, because that meant there was likely to be damage to the nerves. 'We'll get you out of here soon. Can you remember what happened?'

'No.'

OK. She'd leave that one for the police to sort out. 'Any passengers in the car?' she asked.

'No, just me,' Harvey said.

Which meant they wouldn't have to do a search and rescue: that was a relief. 'I'm going to talk to my station manager about the best way to get you out. I'll be back as soon as I can, OK?'

'Don't leave me.' His breath hitched. 'Please, don't leave me here. I—I don't want to be alone. Please.'

She slid a hand through the gap between the door and the seat and touched his face, comforting him. 'Hey. I'll be back before you know it. Promise. We'll get you out of there, love.'

Ray was already assessing the vehicle when she went to report to him. 'Lorry driver's in shock and sitting on the hard shoulder with a space blanket; car driver possible c-spine injury, query crush injuries but at the moment he can feel his legs. I can't get into the front on either side.'

'OK. When the ambo crew's here, we'll see whether they can work with what they have or if they need us to open the car. We'll stabilise the vehicle for now.'

'I'll keep talking to him,' Kelsey said. 'Let him know what's going on.'

She'd just leaned into the back of the car and reassured Harvey that they were going to make the care safe so it

wouldn't move and jolt him or cause him further injury
when a hand rested in the dip of her back. A touch she recognised. A touch that melted away her tension.

'I wondered if you'd be here. How's it going, Kels?'

Kelsey felt a jolt of pleasure as she heard Matt's voice.
All the paramedics she worked with were good, but Matt
had something extra. And it wasn't just bias because she'd
shared a house with him for eighteen months and he was
officially her best friend. There was something about him.
Something calming—as if he could take the weight of the
whole world and keep you safe, and still keep smiling.
Right now, he was the person she wanted to see more than
anyone else in the world.

'Cavalry's arrived,' she told Harvey with a smile. 'Want
the good news or the good news?'

'Uh-huh.'

'You've got one of the best paramedics in the area to treat
you,' she told him. 'I'm just going to get out of his way so
he can have a proper look at you, but I'll be right here beside
him.' Where she often was: because they made a great team.
Between them, they could get casualties out fast and stabilise them. Save lives. She straightened up and drew Matt
back out of Harvey's earshot. 'His name's Harvey. He's
talking—but not as much as he was. He's complained of
pain in his neck and his legs. I can't tell if he's bleeding or
not—there's too much in the way for me to see any external
haemorrhage—but I don't like his colour.'

'Better get him out fast once we've got a spinal board
on him,' Matt said.

Kelsey turned to Matt's crew partner. 'Dale, the lorry
driver's going into shock but his breathing's fine, he was
talking lucidly, and I've got him sitting on the hard
shoulder in a space blanket. I promised him I'd be back,

but…' She gestured to the car. 'The driver's in a bit of a mess. And he's scared as hell. I couldn't really leave him.'

'There isn't enough space for two of us to work here, so can you go to see the lorry driver?' Matt asked his crew partner.

'Sure,' Dale said, and headed for the hard shoulder.

Ray came over. 'The car's stabilised, Matt. Just tell us if you need more access.'

'Will do. Thanks, Ray.' Matt slid into the back of the car and introduced himself quickly to Harvey. 'I'm going to put a neck collar on you to keep your spine nice and stable.' He assessed the situation swiftly. 'They're going to need to cut you out so Dale—that's my crew partner—and I can move you safely.'

'Mmm,' Harvey mumbled.

Kelsey and Matt exchanged a glance as he withdrew.

'How fast can you do it?' Matt asked.

'Ten, fifteen minutes,' Kelsey said, 'but it's going to be noisy.'

He nodded. 'I'll get the collar on him while you lot get the rams and spreaders sorted. Then I'll sit in the back with him and keep him talking while you cut him out.'

'You'll never squeeze into the back,' Kelsey said. 'I'm smaller than you—I'll fit better. Why don't I sit in there and protect him with the shield while the lads do the cutting? If his condition changes, I'll give you a yell.'

'OK. Thanks.' He smiled at her.

By the time Matt had put the collar on Harvey, the cutting equipment was ready. 'OK for me to go in the back?' Kelsey asked Ray.

At his nod, she grabbed the blue tear-shaped plastic shield and slid into the back of the car.

'Harvey, we're going to cut you out so the paramedics

have got enough space to treat you. It's going to be noisy,' she warned, 'but I'm here with you. And I'm going to put this shield up so you won't get any glass in your face or anything.' In the past, windscreens had simply popped out; in modern cars, the windscreens were bonded to the vehicle and had to be cut through.

'It sounds scary,' she said. 'But I promise you, you'll be fine. Nothing's going to hurt you.'

'Do this a lot?'

He sounded slightly slurred. 'A few times,' Kelsey said. 'And I've been cut out of a car myself. So I know what it feels like to be sitting where you are.'

The noise. The splintering glass. The fear that something was going to go wrong and you'd be hurt even more. The absolute conviction that you were going to die and you weren't going to get the chance to say goodbye to the people who mattered.

Again, she damped down the memories. Now wasn't the time. 'You'll be out of here really soon,' she said.

Though every second seemed to drag. The noise felt as if it was never going to stop. And all the while she kept talking to Harvey, trying to get him to respond.

As soon as the fire crew had finished getting the access the paramedics needed, she climbed out of the car and Matt and Dale took over.

'I want to get some fluids into him,' Matt said. 'He's going into shock. Kels, can you do us a favour?'

'Sure.' It was firefighter protocol for the crew to help other teams where they were needed most once they'd done their own job in making sure the area was safe. And she'd worked with Matt enough times to know what he wanted her to do. 'Hold the drip and squeeze the bag so you can get the fluids in faster?'

He blew her a kiss. 'Perfect answer. We'll make a paramedic of you yet.'

'Not before we make a firefighter out of you,' she retorted with a grin.

'Oi, do you mind? I'm not losing my best partner ever,' Dale cut in. 'No, we'd rather pinch you for our team, Brains. Then we might stand a chance in the pub quiz.'

'No way. Your uniform's not as sexy as mine.' She winked at him. 'Isn't that right, Harvey? Firefighters are sexier than paramedics?'

Their patient mumbled something none of them could understand. Matt raised an eyebrow and put the line in Harvey's arm and directed Kelsey to start squeezing the fluid through. Calm, professional, no hint of panic in his voice—even though Kelsey could tell from the look on his face that Harvey was in for a rough time.

But when it came to moving him… 'His leg's stuck,' Matt said grimly.

'What do you need—dashboard roll or pedal release?' Kelsey asked.

'Pedals.'

'OK. I can do that.' She handed the drip bag back to him and grabbed the cutters. She slid the shield over Harvey's legs to protect him, then used the cutters to snap the pedal that had trapped Harvey's foot.

'Remind me not to arm-wrestle you,' Matt said as she gently moved the pedal away to allow Matt to finish getting Harvey out of the car.

'Chicken,' she teased.

'I'd be chicken, too,' Dale said with a grin.

She put her hands on her hips and tutted. 'Weaklings, the pair of you.'

'Yeah, yeah. But thanks for your help, Kels.' Matt's

eyes crinkled at the corners. Amazing blue eyes, the colour of a summer evening sky. Eyes that had reputedly melted every female's heart at the hospital, though Matt rarely dated—a fact which shouldn't have pleased Kelsey nearly as much as it did.

'Any time.' She smiled back at him. 'See you later.'

'And don't forget it's your turn to cook tonight,' he reminded her as he and Dale gently manoeuvred Harvey onto the stretcher.

Kelsey grimaced. Cooking was such a waste of time. Spending hours fiddling about with food when it would all be eaten within ten minutes. 'It's Friday. I'll bring a take-away home.'

'I suppose at least you can't burn that,' Matt said, laughing, as he headed for the ambulance.

'Ah, but if she does at least she's a trained firefighter and can put out the blaze,' Joe teased, walking over to them. 'Ready, Brains?'

'Sure,' Kelsey said as the ambulance doors closed behind Matt.

'So have you two finally seen the light and got together?' Joe asked as they headed back to the fire engine.

'Don't be so daft.' She waved his comment aside. 'We're just friends. *Good* friends.'

Joe made a face that told her he didn't believe a word of it.

She rolled her eyes. 'It *is* possible for men and women to be just friends, you know. Look at you and me.'

'That's different,' Joe said, sounding smug. 'We're colleagues.'

'Matt's like my brother,' Kelsey protested.

'Hmm. I don't look at my sister like that. And she doesn't look at me like that either.'

'Like what?' she asked.

Joe shrugged. 'Work it out for yourself, Brains.'

She flapped a hand at him again. 'Maggie's obviously dragged you to too many girly films lately. You're fantasising.'

'You,' Joe said sweetly, 'need to come back from Egypt.'

'What?'

'Out of denial. De Nile,' he added, to ram his point home further.

Kelsey didn't dignify the corny old joke with a reply. Of course she wasn't in love—or even lust—with Matt Fraser. She had red blood in her veins so, just like any other woman, she could appreciate how good-looking he was. Blond, slightly shaggy hair; broad shoulders and toned body from all the physical work he did; stunning blue eyes and a smile that brightened any room. But it was the same way she'd appreciate a good-looking guy in a TV ad. Matt was her best friend. Her housemate. And that was all.

Wasn't it?

CHAPTER TWO

'HARVEY MITCHELL, aged thirty-two. Cut out of a car at RTC.' Matt went through the rest of the handover to the registrar on the way through to Resus, detailing the action they'd taken at the scene and the pain relief they'd given already. 'Query c-spine injury, complained of pains in leg, and his foot was trapped under a pedal.'

'OK, we'll take it from here.' Janice Horton, the registrar, smiled at him. 'Cheers, Matt.'

'Pleasure.' He smiled back. 'And this time I'm crossing my fingers that I actually get to drink my coffee before the next shout.'

'Come and sneak into our rest room and I'll get you a mug of coffee. Just let me know how you take it,' the nurse walking out of Resus said. She smiled at him. 'I'm Shona Barton, by the way. Staff nurse. I started here yesterday.'

'Matt Fraser, and this is Dale Lewis.' He smiled back at her. 'Thanks for the offer, love, but it's Friday afternoon so I reckon you're just about to be rushed off your feet.'

'Maybe we could have a drink later, then?'

Was it his imagination, or had she just wiggled her hips at him?

Shona was pretty, in a pocket Venus sort of way. Blonde

hair that she'd pinned back but which obviously fell almost
to her waist if she wore it down. And the trousers and tunic
she wore did absolutely nothing to disguise her curves.
Lush curves. Curves that would have most of the ambulance crew on their knees and panting.

And she'd just asked him out.

Oh, hell. How could he say no without sounding snotty?
And he had to be very careful what he said—rumours ripped
through the hospital like wildfire, so if he claimed he was
already spoken for there would be all kinds of speculation.
Speculation he could do without. He didn't *need* a love life.
He had his job, and that was enough for him. 'Thanks for the
offer, Shona, but I'm afraid I'm already doing something tonight.' Sleeping. On his own. But she didn't need to know that.

'Another time?'

'Yeah, maybe. You know how it is.' He gave her an
apologetic smile. 'Shifts never matching up.' Though his
happened to match Kelsey's exactly. Two days, two nights
and four off. His shifts weren't quite the same as hers—
seven in the morning until six at night for days, whereas
she worked from nine until six. He worked six at night until
seven in the morning for nights, whereas she worked from
six until nine—but they were a pretty good fit.

'I could always swap shifts to match yours,' Shona suggested.

Damn. He hadn't thought of that. 'Yeah. Maybe.' Like
not. 'I'd better sort out my paperwork. Catch you later.'

'Paperwork?' Dale asked softly, once they were on the
way back to the ambulance station.

'Uh. Yeah.' Matt ignored his crew partner's raised
eyebrow. And Dale let him change the subject—but the rest
of the crew at the station had plenty to say when they heard
the gossip.

'You've got to be kidding! He turned *Venus* down?' Kirk asked.

Matt frowned. Had he missed something? 'Who's Venus?'

Dale rolled his eyes. 'You know. Long blonde hair. All curves. Sweet, sweet smile. Has all the single male paramedics on their knees begging for a date—and probably half the doctors in the hospital as well.'

Obviously he still looked blank, because Kirk sighed. 'The new nurse in the emergency department,' he added. 'The gorgeous one. The one that started yesterday. The one that apparently asked you out this afternoon.'

'Oh. Shona, you mean.'

'And you said no?' Kirk shook his head. 'Oh, dearie me. Maybe Dale should hook you up to the ECG before your next shout.'

Matt took a swig of his coffee. 'What are you on about?'

'Someone needs to check you still have a pulse,' Kirk retorted.

'Course he's got a pulse,' Dale said.

Kirk scoffed. 'I dunno. If he's turning down gorgeous women like that…'

'Look, not everyone wants to date six different women a week,' Matt said.

'Better than not dating at all,' Kirk sniped.

Matt knew if he responded, the situation would escalate and turn ugly. So he ignored the comment and carried on going through his paperwork.

But Kirk was clearly spoiling for an argument. 'What's the matter? Doesn't Venus match up to the girl of your dreams?' he asked.

'Probably not,' Matt said coolly.

Kirk started whistling the theme from *Trumpton*, a classic children's animated TV series about a fire brigade, which had given the paramedics an affectionate nickname for their local fire service.

Matt, knowing exactly what his colleague was getting at, sighed. 'I don't think so.'

'He's right,' Dale said to Kirk. 'Sure, he lives with Kelsey—but, nah, he doesn't fancy her. She's like his sister.'

'Best friend, actually,' Matt pointed out. 'Off limits.'

Kirk rubbed his chin. 'She's not like Venus—too skinny, too tall, too serious—but, yeah, I'd buy the Trumptons' charity calendar this year if Kelsey was on it.' He grinned and waggled his eyebrows. 'Especially if she was topless. Or better. I wouldn't mind seeing her in nothing but a fire helmet.'

The reflex that had Matt's right hand balling into a fist shocked him. He made an effort to relax his hand. 'Kels wouldn't do that sort of thing.'

'Pity.' Kirk's grin broadened. 'They'd sell truckloads if she did.'

'Hmm,' was all Matt trusted himself to say. And if Kirk ever asked Kelsey out, Matt would make damned sure that Kelsey said no. Kirk wasn't good enough for her. Wasn't anywhere *near* good enough for her. He didn't want Kirk's grubby paws touching Kelsey. Didn't want *anyone* touching Kelsey, actually. But he shoved that thought to the back of his mind.

To his relief, there was a call on his intercom. 'We'd better get going. I'll drive so you can finish your coffee,' he said to Dale. He climbed into the driver's side of their ambulance and radioed back to Control. 'On our way.'

'You OK?' Dale asked as Matt drove off.

Matt shrugged. 'Sure. Why wouldn't I be?'

Dale shifted in his seat. 'Teasing you about Kelsey.'

'Doesn't bother me.'

'I saw your hands,' Dale said softly, 'when Kirk made

that remark about the calendar. Look, cut him some slack. He's still hurting about his divorce. That's why he's desperate to date as many women as he can. To prove he's not a complete loser.'

'Hmm,' was all Matt said.

Dale sighed. 'Ow. I know. You've already been there. Not a loser, I mean. And not divorced. But you were as good as married to Cassie. And I'm putting my size twelves in it today, big time. I'm sorry.'

'No worries. I'm over it now.' It had taken Matt nearly eighteen months to lick his wounds. They'd healed. He and Cassie hadn't been right for each other anyway. She hadn't understood his job or why he didn't mind the unsocial hours; and he hadn't wanted to change and fit into her world, swap the job he loved for one where he didn't feel alive and as if he was making a difference.

'As for Kelsey—I mean, I like her. We all do.'

Matt heard what Dale wasn't saying. 'But?'

'But you're storing yourself up a hell of a lot of heartache if you've fallen for her, Matt. She doesn't do serious relationships. She parties hard—she's the first one at the end of a pizza night out to suggest going on to a club—but she doesn't let anyone close. You know the score.'

Nobody serious since Danny. Most of the time Matt and Kelsey didn't talk about it. But on the rare occasions when they did, Kelsey was adamant. She liked her life just as it was. And Matt could understand that. Life as it was suited him, too.

'I haven't fallen for her,' Matt said.

Dale's response was a measured 'Hmm'.

And then they were at the shout so the conversation was lost.

By the time they'd checked out the woman who'd called

999 with chest pains, taken an ECG and then brought her into the emergency department for further tests and observation, it was forgotten about. All the same, Matt was thoughtful as he cycled home at the end of his shift. Had he fallen for Kelsey? Was she the girl of his dreams?

She was his best friend. His housemate. They swapped horror stories at the end of their shifts and they knew when the other needed a hug and a shared tub of ice cream. They shared the same set of friends, went out with the same crowds—the crews at the ambulance station all knew her, and the crews at the fire station all knew him. As Dale had said, Kelsey partied hard but she almost never dated—and when she did date, she didn't stay out all night or bring anyone home.

Matt didn't date much either, but it went with the job. Long hours, tough calls and a social life that sometimes had to take second place to your job. If you were in the middle of a shout when your shift ended, you couldn't just dump your patient and tell them to wait for the next crew. That was the whole thing about being an emergency service. And if there was a major incident, even if you were off shift you'd go in and do your bit. It went with the territory. He'd already learned that the hard way when he'd had to make the choice between his fiancée and his job.

His job had won.

All the same… A picture of Kelsey flashed into his mind. Short hair, cheeky grin, sparkling grey eyes. Kirk had called her tall and skinny—no, that wasn't true. Matt had trained in the gym with her enough times when they had been on nights and wanted to wind down at the end of their shifts. Tall, yes; slender, yes; but Kelsey definitely had curves. And the way she looked in a plain black swimsuit was enough to make any man's blood pressure rise a couple of notches.

He shook himself. He was *not* about to wreck a seriously good relationship by dating her. Kelsey was his sounding board. The person he'd listen to at three in the morning if she needed him—and he knew that she'd do exactly the same for him. His best friend. His housemate. Dating each other would be a disaster. One of them would end up having to find a new place to live. No, it was best to keep things as they were.

The open windows told Kelsey that Matt was home. Good. So she wasn't going to have to juggle her briefcase and the carrier bag full of take-away Indian food and use her front-door key at the same time. She pushed down the handle of the front door with her elbow and swung her hip to open the door. Perfect. She closed the door with another swing of her hips.

Matt appeared in the living-room doorway. 'A normal person would ring the doorbell. Or at least accept help.'

'You can help if you want to.' She grinned and handed him the carrier bag. 'Dinner is served, m'lord.'

'Good. I'm starving. I nearly raided your chocolate stash.'

'You'd better not have done.' She set her briefcase on the floor and followed him into the kitchen. 'I'm studying tonight.' Although the fire service had changed their training so you didn't have to sit a raft of promotional exams any more, you still needed to know the theory and technical details, so you could prove that you knew what you were doing and met the competencies to go up to the next grade. Which meant studying. 'I *need* that chocolate,' she added.

'It's Friday night. Aren't you going out?'

'Not tonight. I want to do a couple of hours' studying and then just chill.' She smiled inwardly when she saw the neatly set table in their kitchen-diner. Typical Matt. All the other people she knew in the emergency services would just take the cardboard off the take-away foil container and dig in with a spoon. Matt was much, much more domesticated. Though, to look at him right now, with his shaggy hair and the fact he needed a shave, nobody would guess it. He looked more like a guitarist in a rock band than a paramedic. He looked sexy as hell.

And she really had to stop thinking about that before she screwed up their friendship. Matt was off limits.

'So how was your day?' he asked, taking the lid off the pilau rice and spooning the rice onto their plates.

'OK. We had a quiet afternoon after that RTC—just a kitchen fire that was out by the time we got there. Did you know, there was a newspaper report today that most RTCs happen between four and seven on a Friday afternoon?'

'I can believe it. Mixture of the "thank God it's Friday" feeling and people being physically tired at the end of the week. Their concentration goes.' Matt beamed when he opened the next lid. 'Oh, you star. Chicken kashmiri. My favourite.'

'And far better than if I'd cooked it for you.'

'Yep. Means we don't have to call your lot to put out the flames in the oven—or my lot to rescue us from the food poisoning afterwards,' he teased.

'Oh, ha, ha.' She walked over to the fridge. 'Two nights, then four blissful days off.' Luckily their shifts were pretty much the same. Her night shifts were slightly longer than Matt's, but at least one of them didn't have to creep around the house on days off while the other was on nights.

'Nearly twenty-four hours until I'm due back in at the station. I could go wild and have a few beers tonight. But I need a clear head to work on my fire management stuff. So I think I'll stick to just the one.' She uncapped two bottles and brought them over to the table. It had taken her six months to persuade Matt that cold beer tasted better from a bottle than a glass. And why make extra washing-up?

He finished dishing up the curry, then lifted his bottle in salute. 'Cheers. Here's to us. Top team.'

'Top team,' she echoed.

Which they were. Since she'd shared the house with Matt, she'd always felt she was coming home, not just going back to rented digs.

Not that she and Matt had *that* type of relationship. They were just friends. Best of friends. Had been ever since he'd moved into the house eighteen months ago, when his engagement to Cassie had broken up and Sarah—the paramedic who'd originally shared the house with Kelsey—had asked her if Matt could use their spare room for a few nights.

But it had worked so well that Matt had stayed. And although Sarah had moved out to live with her boyfriend in London a few months ago, Matt and Kelsey hadn't bothered replacing the third person in the house. It was comfortable, just the two of them.

Cassie had been crazy, Kelsey thought. She really couldn't have had any idea what she had missed. What she had given up. A smart, funny guy who was good at his job, respected by everyone—and was domesticated into the bargain.

Mr Perfect.

Except Kelsey wasn't going to let herself take that last step. Been there, done that. She wasn't giving herself the chance ever again to lose anyone who mattered to her. Besides, why wreck the best relationship she'd ever had for a short-term fling?

'Penny for them?' Matt asked.

Oh, no. She wasn't going to tell him that. She smiled. 'Nothing much. How was your day, by the way?'

'Usual summer Friday. One case of heatstroke in the park; one bad back from someone who'd overdone it in the garden yesterday and couldn't even get out of bed; then a maternataxi case.'

Paramedic jargon for a pregnant woman who'd left it way too late to ring the maternity unit to say she was having contractions, then had to be rushed to hospital in an ambulance—and Kelsey knew that Matt had delivered a few babies in his time.

'Then it was your RTA—'

'RTC,' Kelsey corrected.

'RTA,' Matt continued with a grin. 'I'm using ambo terminology, not fire. After you, there was a possible heart attack, and then it was the end of my shift. Did you have a lousy day before the RTA?'

'School safety visit this morning, one out-of-control barbecue at lunchtime—can you believe that people actually think it's a good idea to throw lighter fuel on top of a lit barbecue?' She flexed her shoulders. 'I enjoyed doing the safety visit.'

'You always do. It's the teacher in you,' Matt said.

'Well, I'm not a teacher any more. Never was, really.' She shrugged. 'I walked out before I qualified.'

'Ever regret it?'

She shook her head. 'I love what I do now. Same as you. You never know what you're going to face when you go on shift. Could be absolutely anything. Could be quiet, could be rushed off your feet—and I wouldn't swap it for anything.'

Sometimes she thought that she got a buzz from the danger—the risks she took were calculated, but her job was still dangerous. Like Matt's. It was one of the reasons Cassie hadn't been able to handle Matt's job—as well as the unsocial hours, there was the fact that he could always be hurt on duty. He had to deal with Friday or Saturday night callouts in the middle of the city, where people had been drinking or doing drugs—the wrong word at the wrong time, and they could react badly. Lash out or put a knife through his ribs.

Then again, Kelsey routinely had to face explosions, flashovers, clearing up dangerous chemicals… It would take someone special to understand why the danger was never uppermost in her mind when she was at work. Her focus was rescuing someone from a bad situation, putting their life back together again. Mending the hurt. Just like Matt did.

When they'd finished dinner, they cleared the table. Kelsey picked up the teatowel, ready to dry the dishes, but Matt took it from her with a smile. 'Leave this. You're studying. Two hours, you said.'

'Ye-es.'

'So why don't I go to the video shop and hire us a good film? We can start watching the film at half-nine—you'll still be in bed by midnight.'

Typical Matt: this was his way of making sure she didn't work too hard, but without nagging her. Thoughtful. She adored him for it. 'Sounds just about perfect,' she said with a smile. 'Thanks, Matt.'

'No worries.' He flapped the teatowel at her. 'Go do your studying. I'll sort this.'

Two hours later, there was a rap on her door.

'Come in.'

'Hey. I have popcorn, a tub of ice cream and that new thriller that went on release today.'

'What flavour ice cream?'

'Strawberry cheesecake.'

Her favourite. Kelsey saved her file and shut down her laptop. 'I'm there.' She followed him downstairs and flopped on the sofa next to him.

The perfect Friday night. A good film, her best friend and her favourite munchies.

'If you guess who did it, just don't tell me,' Matt said.

'As if I would,' she teased. She rolled her shoulders, easing the kinks out of them.

'You study in the wrong position, you know. Slumped over your desk. It's hardly surprising you get backache. Come here and I'll sort that out for you.' He nudged her round so that her back was to him, and began massaging her shoulders.

'Mmm.' Kelsey almost purred with pleasure. He knew just the right spot to touch her. 'If you ever decide you've had enough of being a paramedic, you could make a fortune as a masseur.'

'But then I'd be stuck in one place, and I'd know exactly what I was doing every day. It's like you said earlier—I get a buzz in never knowing what I'm going to face when I go on shift. Though I don't need to explain that to you. You're the same.'

'Yeah.' And it was good. Living on the edge. Making a real difference to people's lives.

'Better?' he asked, just resting his hands lightly on her shoulders.

For a moment she was tempted to say no. So he'd continue touching her. And then maybe, if she leaned back against him, he'd let his hands slip lower to cup her breasts and—

No. Oh, hell. She shouldn't have listened to Joe earlier that day. Having to face a traffic accident and cut someone out of a car had rattled her a bit, stirred up the feelings she normally kept compartmentalised and locked away. And,

good as sex would undoubtedly be with Matt, she wasn't
going to mess things up between them for the sake of one
night's comfort.

She shook herself mentally. 'Much better, thanks. And
for that you get first dibs on the ice cream.'

And she wasn't going to watch the spoon going up to
his mouth and wonder what his mouth might feel like
against hers.

At all.

CHAPTER THREE

EVERYTHING was fine until the following Friday afternoon. A quarter to four. It had been quiet all day—too quiet—and then there was the familiar warble before the Tannoy message. 'Turnout, vehicles 5 and 57. Fire at Bannington Primary School. Query trapped people.'

The primary school was about ten miles from the city centre. Kelsey's crew had talked to the kids there about fire safety only last week. And it was the school Ray's daughter attended—Finn had been delighted, last week, that her dad had brought his fire engine.

Please, God, let it be minor damage, Kelsey begged silently. Let it be a fire in a wastebin or something. Let it be something we can put out. Let nobody be hurt.

She'd never had to deal with a school fire before. Sure, she'd rescued kids from the back of a smashed-up car or from a small house fire, but she'd never faced anything like this. Even the factory fire she'd attended last year hadn't worried her that much: although some workers had been trapped, they'd been able to follow instructions and she'd known it would work out just fine. There'd been minor burns and smoke inhalation, nothing too major. But with kids there was always the problem that they wouldn't understand or they'd be too frightened to do what you told them. And they weren't physically as able to deal with smoke inhalation and the heat of a raging fire as well as adults did.

Ray looked grim as the fire engine sped on its way out of the city. Kelsey could guess what was going through his mind and leaned forward, resting her hand on his shoulder. 'Guv, school finishes at three. The kids will all have gone home. Finn will be fine.'

'There's after-school club for the kids whose parents are still at work,' Ray said tersely. 'I know Finn won't be there, but some of her friends might be.'

'Hey. Might even be a false alarm—like it usually is when we get a callout to the university,' Paul said.

'Let's hope,' Ray said, his voice clipped. 'Police and the ambo team have been called as well.'

But when they turned into School Road, they could see smoke.

Ray swore. 'They don't have a sprinkler system, except in the new block.'

Kelsey remembered that the main part of the school was Victorian, a rambling building that had grown along with the urban sprawl of the town. It was full of corridors and small rooms and with varying levels to the floor. The kind of building that always worried firefighters because the layout wasn't logical and the access points weren't always clear. She also knew that Ray, as a school governor, had been agitating to get sprinklers fitted to the main building but the project had been tied up in arguments between the planning authority and the education authority over listed building regulations. There had been hold-up after hold-up over the proposed changes to the building while they had tried to reach a compromise that would satisfy both areas. With sprinklers, the fire would be less serious. Without, who knew what they'd face?

'Guv, they've probably got everyone out. The teachers'll be waiting in the playground, having ticked all the kids' names off,' Kelsey suggested.

'Maybe. But you know as well as I do that the worst time for us is after-school club—the numbers attending vary, and some of the kids there don't go there full time so they don't really know the layout of the building. It's not like daytime where everyone knows exactly what's going on. Right, everyone. Full PPE on.' Personal protective equipment—because this could easily turn nasty. 'Joe, stay with the vehicle.'

'Right, guv,' Joe said as he parked the fire engine.

'Paul, I want you as BAECO.' The BAECO, or breathing apparatus entry co-ordinator, kept the control board with all the firefighters' tallies in place, so he knew who was in the building, how long they'd been in there and when they'd need to be out again.

'Right, guv,' Paul said.

'Kelsey, you and Mark set the hydrant and get extra water while the other crew start putting water on the blaze—the tanks aren't going to be enough for this.' Each fire engine carried eighteen hundred litres of water in its tanks—enough to deal with a small bedroom fire in a house, but not enough for what could potentially be a huge blaze.

'Right, guv,' they chorused.

The fire alarm was shrilling; there were four adults and a number of children marshalled on the grass at the side of the building furthest from the fire.

One of them came straight over to the fire crew. Clearly the head or one of Finn's teachers, Kelsey thought from the way she greeted Ray—she obviously knew him.

'What happened, Brenda?' he asked.

'I heard a bang, then the smoke detectors went off. I think the boiler must have exploded,' Brenda said. 'I've got one of the after-school groups out but the other's cut off in the far end. One teacher, two assistants and around twenty kids.'

Ray called in to Control. 'I want another engine in and as many BA sets as you can give me,' he said. When fighting a fire, the crew went through breathing apparatus sets more quickly than usual, so they needed as many available as possible. 'We've got three adults and twenty or so kids trapped. We're going to get them out and start on the blaze.' He turned back to Brenda. 'Any flammable stuff we need to know about?'

'Most of the classrooms have art materials. Paper, glue, paint and the like. There's the chemistry stuff in the lab, but that's at the far end.'

'Near the trapped kids. So far, not near the fire. OK, we'll bear that in mind.' He nodded and turned to the crew. 'We'll split the building into three sectors. Andy and Neil, I want you two in sector one where the boiler is. Pete and Tom, I want you in sector two, the classrooms between the boiler room and the toilets in the middle of the school. Kelsey and Mark, I want you in sector three—the far end of the school. It doesn't look as if the fire's there yet so get them out as quickly as you can. We'll see how the fire's going after that, and I might need you to work on the science lab.'

They all checked in with Paul, handing him the tallies from their breathing apparatus sets. He slotted them into the board, wrote their names and the time in beside them, checked the pressure of the oxygen cylinders and used the dial to work out the time when they needed to be out, and marked that on the grid next to it.

Kelsey and Mark took axes with them and headed for the classroom at the far end.

'Has to be a window,' Mark said.

The windows were tall and narrow, typically Victorian. 'I'm thinner than you,' Kelsey said when they'd cleared the glass from one of the frames. 'Makes sense for me to go in.' She unbuckled her breathing apparatus.

'What the hell are you doing?' Mark demanded, sounding shocked.

'There's no smoke in the classroom right now so I don't need my BA set—and, anyway, it's easier for me to climb through the window without the extra bulk, let alone carrying the thirty pounds of kit,' Kelsey said. 'Give us a leg up.'

'But, Brains—'

'No time to argue. Let's get them out.'

'OK, but I'm putting the BA set through after you. And you make sure you put it on when you get back in,' he demanded, 'even if you don't have the mask on.'

'Deal.' She clambered onto the window-sill with Mark's help and squeezed through the gap, then took the breathing apparatus he pushed through after her. 'Hi, my name's Kelsey. You might remember me from last week when Finn's dad brought the fire engine in,' she said, smiling at the children. 'Now, we're going to have to go out of the room a different way today, because we can't use the door.' No smoke was seeping through it yet, but there were no guarantees it would stay that way. 'Can you all be brave for me?'

Some of the younger ones were sobbing. The sound ripped at her but she forced herself to ignore it. She had a job to do. And her first duty was to calm everyone right down. Giving in to her emotions and crying or screaming herself would just scare everyone and make it harder to get them out.

'Hey, give us a smile. Makes it easier to lift you,' she

said. She turned to the three adults, who'd been trying to keep the children calm. 'I need one of you to help me lift the children through the window, and two of you outside— one to help lift them out into the playground and one to check off the names.'

'I'm Jane, the classroom assistant. I'll stay inside,' the youngest one said immediately.

'Thanks. Can you get them all to line up, littlest at the front? And can you two help me get a table to the window?' she asked the other two adults.

Together, they dragged a table to the window. The two older women clambered onto the table, squeezed through the window and were helped down by Mark. Then, between them, Kelsey and Jane lifted the children one at a time onto the table and handed them through the window into Mark's waiting arms.

'Just think, you can tell your mum what an exciting day you've had and how you've climbed through the window like a real firefighter,' Kelsey said, trying to reassure the children.

A couple of the kids were still crying.

'But it's *not* exciting. There's a fire, we're trapped and we're all going to die!' one of the older kids said, his voice shrill with panic.

'There's a fire, yes. But I'm a firefighter and I'm going to put the blaze out,' she told him calmly. 'You can't go through the door, but you're not trapped because we're lifting you out through the window. And you are most definitely not going to die. Not when Yellow Watch is here.'

'Finn's daddy is a fireman,' one of them piped up.

'That's right. He's a very good fireman. And he's my boss. So you're all going to be absolutely fine,' Kelsey reassured her, continuing to lift the children out through the window one by one. 'Just stay still so we can get you through safely, because there's broken glass around here and I don't want any of you to get cut.'

But the boy who'd panicked earlier struggled as she lifted him through the window. Immediately, he cried out. 'My leg!'

He was wearing shorts, so the streak of blood was visible on his leg immediately. Quite a deep cut, from the jagged glass around the smashed window—and there was a chance that there was some glass in the wound. At least it wasn't spurting blood, she thought, so he hadn't nicked an artery. 'OK, sweetheart, we'll sort you out. Just hold still and we'll get you out to safety. I know it hurts, but one of the ambulance team will look at your leg and make sure you're OK. And I think they have bravery awards for special boys,' she soothed. 'Mark, is the ambo team here yet?'

'We certainly are,' a deep voice informed her.

Matt. She didn't even need to look to know it was him. And suddenly the tension in her shoulders began to ease. Everything was going to be fine: there was nobody she'd trust more for support. She grinned. 'Hey. What kept you, slowcoach?'

'We don't have the same go-faster stripes as your lot,' he teased back. 'You OK, Kels?'

'Sure. Four more to go and we're out of here. Can you look at this young man's leg for me? And I think he might need a bravery award as well.'

'Sounds about right. Come on, mate, I'll carry you over to the ambulance,' Matt said, taking the child from her. 'We'll sort out that cut and get you a special award.'

When she and Jane had handed the last child through, Kelsey asked, 'That's definitely everyone?'

Jane nodded. 'I think so.'

'Good. Through you go.' Kelsey helped her through the

window into Mark's arms. She'd pushed her BA set back through to Mark and was halfway through the gap in the window herself—protected by her gloves and fire gear—when one of the children called, 'Where's Mikey and Lucy?'

Ah, hell. She should've thought. In situations like these, the kids were usually better at knowing who was there and who wasn't than the teachers—they remembered if their friend was in late because they'd been to the dentist, or had gone home early because they'd been sick. Registers were only accurate at the time they were taken—all sorts of things could change during the school day.

The class teacher did a head count and was clearly running through the register in her mind. 'They're not here.'

'They were definitely in today?' At the teacher's nod, Kelsey asked, 'Where are they likely to be?'

'Heaven knows with Mikey—he's never still for more than three seconds,' the teacher said, sounding grim.

'You're sure he isn't out there and hasn't just slipped out of the line and gone onto the playground or something?'

The teacher shook her head. 'They're all strictly in line, except Edward, who's in the ambulance having his leg patched up.'

'Right. I'll go back and check the cupboards,' Kelsey said. Sometimes a fire scared kids so much that they'd hide in a confined space. 'Or maybe they've gone to the toilet. I'll check. What do they look like?'

'Mikey's tall and skinny, blond hair, and Lucy's small and dark-haired,' Jane told her. 'I'll come with you.'

Kelsey shook her head. 'No, it's too dangerous. Stay there and see if any of the kids remember them disappearing, or if they heard where Mikey or Lucy was planning to go. Any news, contact me on my radio. Where are the toilets?'

'Out of the door, turn right, and they're on the left-hand side at the end of the corridor.'

Near the flames. OK. Kelsey climbed back through the window. 'Mark, give me the BA set. The pressure's at 300 so I've got forty minutes.'

He handed the set through. 'Forty minutes in normal conditions—but you know it's less than that in a fire. I want you on your way back when the pressure's down to 200.' Which was less than halfway through the cylinder, because she needed to leave a safety margin. You had to be prepared for anything in a fire. 'Keep in radio contact, and as soon as you're in a compartment with smoke do a left-hand search from the doorway,' Mark added.

A left-hand search meant keeping her left hand in contact with the wall. Then, if she wasn't back to her starting point when the pressure in her oxygen tank reached 200, she'd turn round so her right hand was against the wall and work her way back. In a smoke-filled room, you couldn't see your hand in front of your face, so working by touch was the only way to get back where you started.

Mikey, who was never still for more than three seconds…tall and skinny and blond… Kelsey remembered him now from Yellow Watch's recent visit to the school. He'd touched everything and fiddled with things, but he'd also been quickwitted and taken everything she'd said on board when she'd shown him round the engine, asked lots of questions and said he really wanted to be a firefighter when he was older. If he managed to contain his energy, he'd be a good one, Kelsey thought.

She put her breathing apparatus set on her back but left the mask off. 'Mikey? Lucy? If you're here, come out. You win the hiding game, but we need to get out of here.'

Silence.

She checked the cupboards in the classroom anyway. Nothing. 'Classroom empty,' she reported into her radio. 'I'm going into the corridor.' Which was full of smoke. 'I'll check the toilets first.' Hopefully the kids would've remembered what they'd said at the talk last week: if you're in a fire, get down because smoke rises.

And it was smoke that killed.

Left-hand search. She put her hand to the wall. Through her gloves, she could feel that the walls were panelled. Not good—because you could think you'd put a blaze out when the fire had actually travelled through the panelling and could break out somewhere else. She'd need to keep an eye out for white smoke, presaging of a flashover.

'Lucy? Mikey?' Her voice was muffled through the mask, but she couldn't risk taking it off. 'Scream if you can hear me. Scream as loud as you can.'

Nothing but the dull roar of the flames.

She made her way through to the toilets. Searched them thoroughly. 'Nothing in the toilets,' she said. 'And all doors in the corridor are closed on the left-hand side. Ask Jane if there's a room Mikey likes most.'

'Roger.' She heard Mark calling to Jane, then he reported back. 'No, the kid could be anywhere.'

'OK. I'll do a room-by-room search.'

'You've got two minutes before you need to turn round and come back,' Mark warned.

'I'm fine.'

'I want you back out of there. We'll get more people in to search each room,' Mark said.

It was frustrating, but she knew he was talking sense. 'OK. Turning round and coming back right-handed.' Her hand trailed along the wall. 'Hang on. I've got an open door here. It wasn't open on my way in. I'm going to check this room.'

'Brains, get *out* of there.'

She couldn't. Not with two kids missing. 'Two minutes. You said I had two minutes. And there's the safety margin on top of that, so I've got loads of time. I'm closing the door behind me. There's only a tiny bit of smoke in here, top of the room.' Smoke always rose. But she needed to keep an eye on it in case the gases at the top of the room were superheated and there was a flashover. 'I'm in the third room between the classroom and the toilets. Send the relief team in and I'll hand over.'

'Paul says get out *now*, Brains.'

'Two minutes,' she repeated stubbornly—though she really wanted five. 'Lucy? Mikey? Are you there? You're not going to be in trouble, I promise. But there's a fire and I just want to get you out safely.'

'Brains, you're better at calculating than the rest of us— you don't even need the dial on a BAECO board to work out how much time you have. You know the drill—if you put yourself in danger we're risking the kids *and* yourself. Get out now,' Mark demanded.

'I'm fine, Mark. And I heard something. I heard someone crying just now. I think they're here in the cupboard and they're too scared to come out.'

'Get out of there, Kelsey.' A different voice this time. Matt's. 'I heard what Mark said. Get *out*. There's another team coming in.'

'I'm fine,' she repeated stubbornly. 'But you stay put because I might be bringing two kids out with smoke inhalation or burns, and I'll need your help.' She took her mask off for a moment. 'Mikey, it's Kelsey—remember me on the fire engine last week? You know me. You're not in trouble, I promise. But I need you to act like a fire-fighter. And firefighters always have to tell each other where they are. I'm here near the door. Where are you? Is Lucy with you?'

The cupboard door opened. Mikey and a little girl were standing there, clutching each other and not moving.

'It's OK, we can get out of here.' The hanging mask was going to be a hindrance. 'I'm putting my mask back on and then we're going to make a run for it, OK?'

She'd just fastened her mask and was halfway across the room when there was an almighty bang. Fire spurted out of the panelling and ripped over the ceiling—and suddenly there was a wall of flame between her and the kids. The fire roared and crackled as it burned up the oxygen in the room; the floor, being wooden, started smouldering. And she couldn't get through the fire to the kids. It was too hot, too fierce, pushing her back. 'Mark, the fire's broken through here. Tell the guv.' She grabbed the fire extinguisher, but it didn't even begin to get through the flames. There was a sink but the water pressure wouldn't be enough to make an impact on the flames. But she could at least grab some cloths, soak them and bundle them round the kids, then haul them through the flames. Please, God, the floor would hold out long enough for her to get them.

It took seconds to find the towels, and seconds more to douse them in cold water.

But the pressure from the fire was too much. She just couldn't get through the wall of flames.

'Get down!' she yelled to the children. 'Get down and put your nose down through the neck of your T-shirts so you're breathing in through the material.' The lower they were, the less likely they'd be to inhale the smoke—the lowest part of the room was always the last to be choked with gases. And breathing through their clothes would at least put a barrier between them and the smoke. Not ideal, but it was the best they could do in the circumstances.

She could hear the children screaming, a high-pitched sound of sheer terror.

Oh, hell, why couldn't she get through? She took a deep breath. OK. If she made a run for it, she'd get through the flames. She'd be able to bundle the wet cloths over the kids. And hopefully the relief team would put the flames out before the smoke was too much. Deep breath in. After three. One, two—

And someone lifted her off her feet.

'No! I've got to—'

'*Out*, Brains.' She couldn't see him through the smoke and his mask, but she recognised Mark's muffled voice. 'You're out of oxygen,' he said.

'Just give me another tank. I can make it through to the kids.'

He didn't argue. Just lifted her higher over his shoulder in the classic fireman's lift, took her down the corridor and pushed her through the smashed window of the classroom they'd just evacuated.

Straight into Matt's arms.

'You bloody idiot, Kelsey!' Matt yelled. 'You put yourself at risk.'

She shook her head. Her throat felt raw but no way was she staying out here. 'Give me a tank. I need to go back. They're trapped. Two kids. I have to—'

'You have to get medical treatment *now*,' Matt cut in, and she realised that he was actually carrying her to his ambulance. Carrying her away from danger. 'You were out of oxygen. You know damned well when it's hot you use up more oxygen than normal. That's why your crew goes through a ton of BA sets when you're fighting a fire. You've inhaled smoke and I bet your throat's hurting like crazy.'

It was—but she wasn't going to admit it. 'I saw them. I nearly had them safe, but the fire broke out,' she rasped. 'I was going to get through the flames. Where are they?'

Before Matt could answer, Ray was striding over towards them, swearing a blue streak. 'What the hell did you think you were doing, Brains?'

'I nearly had them. And I was in radio contact the whole time.'

'Yes, but you didn't do what you were told. You put yourself and other crew members in danger.'

'Where are the kids? What's going on?'

'Stay put and let Matt check you over. That's an *order*.'

OK. She'd let Matt check her over, and then she was going back in.

Then she realised that Matt was still cradling her in his arms. As if she were a precious piece of china. 'You can put me down now,' she muttered. 'I can stand on my own two feet.'

He stared at her, looking shocked. Clearly he'd been holding her in his arms without realising what he was doing. In silence, he set her back on her feet and walked with her over to the ambulance.

By the time Matt had checked her over, Mark and the other crew were back out and had been replaced by the relief team. There were four more engines here now. Steam billowed upwards, mingling with the choking black smoke. And still the flames licked through the building. Still they roared. Still the heat blistered the air.

'Mark, did you get the kids out?' she asked urgently.

'No. We couldn't hear anyone in there either.'

'Things are always muffled in the middle of a fire. The kids might be too scared to make a sound.'

'Yeah.' But his face said he didn't believe it. That there was another reason why the kids were silent. A much, much worse reason. Especially when the smoke was thick and choking.

Then there was a shout as two firefighters ran towards them, carrying small bodies.

'We've put oxygen on them,' one of the firefighters said.

It was what he didn't say that Kelsey heard. The but. A *big* but. They didn't hold out much hope. The smoke and the heat might have taken too much of a toll on the small bodies.

Matt and Dale put the children straight in the ambulance; Matt stayed in the back, already checking them over, while Dale slammed the doors and scrambled into the driver's seat. Siren going, the ambulance left the site.

'Oh, God. I nearly got them out safely. Nearly,' Kelsey whispered. 'They've got to be all right.' Please. They had to be all right.

CHAPTER FOUR

FOUR hours later, the fire was out. The building was blackened and charred in places, there was the smell of wet embers everywhere, and a mixture of smoke and steam hung in the air. The job was done—but the crew found no satisfaction in it. Not when two small lives hung in the balance.

Even though Kelsey had a shower and washed her hair when she got back to the fire station, she could still smell the smoke. Taste it. Feel it in her eyes. Feel it in the back of her throat.

She couldn't stand the waiting any more. She needed to know. She called the hospital and got through to the reception desk in the emergency department. 'I wondered if you could tell me how Mikey and Lucy are, the two kids brought in from the school fire?'

'Are you a relative?' the receptionist asked.

'No, I'm one of the firefighters.' The one who hadn't got them out in time.

'Sorry. I'm afraid we can't give out information over the phone.'

Well, it was what she'd expected. 'Thanks anyway.' But there was another way she could find out. Someone else who *could* tell her. She speed-dialled Matt's mobile number. Please, don't let him be driving or in the hospital, when his phone would be diverted to his voicemail.

Well, it shouldn't be. She'd ended up working past the end of her shift. He should be home now—or even if he'd gone out with the crew for a Friday evening post-shift drink, he'd have his mobile on.

She hoped.

To her relief, he answered his mobile within three rings. 'Matt Fraser.'

'Hey. It's me.'

'Is the fire out, or are you just having a break and change of crews?'

She smiled. Clearly he'd remembered that firefighters were relieved after a four-hour stint and took a break—a wash, change and something to eat and drink, then back at the front again. Well, he should know after eighteen months of sharing a house with her. 'It's out.'

'Good. You on your way home now?'

'Yeah.' She took a deep breath. 'Matt, I called the hospital. They wouldn't tell me. Do you know how the kids are doing?'

'Yes.' There was a long, long pause that told her everything she didn't want to know. 'I'm sorry. They didn't make it.'

She swore. 'If I'd found them thirty seconds earlier—'

'It's not your fault, Kels. It really isn't.'

So why did it feel that it was?

'You did your best. So did Dale and I, on our way to the hospital. And the resus team when we got to the emergency department. But it wasn't anybody's fault. Who could have guessed that the boiler was going to go up like that? Or that the fire would spread that fast? Or that the kids had slipped out from the after-school club into another room and would hide in a cupboard when the fire alarm went off?'

'Mmm.' She didn't trust herself to speak. Her eyes felt sore and gritty, and not just from exposure to smoke and heat.

'Kels.' His voice was soft, understanding. Like a hug down the phone line. Warm and strong and comforting. And how she wished he was right in front of her, holding her close. 'Don't beat yourself up. You've had four hours of hard work, carrying nearly thirty pounds of kit on your back. You must be shattered. And it was a nightmare job. It's the first time you've been to a fire at a school, isn't it?'

'Yeah.'

He pressed on. 'The first time you've not been able to save a child.'

She dragged in a breath. 'Yeah,' she whispered. She'd been to a couple of big blazes where they'd lost people, but she'd never been to a fire where they'd lost a child. Two children. One of whom she actually *knew*, from her fire prevention work at the school. She'd never have believed it would hurt so much. Or that it would affect her like this. She was a trained professional. She wasn't supposed to feel this way.

'It's your first one, of course you'll be feeling emotional. Anyone would, in your shoes. I remember the first time I couldn't save a kid in a car crash and it hit me pretty hard. Look, I'm at home. I'll come and pick you up.'

'No. I'm fine,' she mumbled. 'Be home soon.' Though when she ended the call, she let the phone drop on the table, propped her elbows on the wood and rested her forehead on her clenched fists. She should have been able to save those kids. She'd failed in her job. She'd been saved from a mangled car in her hour of need—but she'd failed to do the same for Mikey and Lucy. She hadn't paid her debt. She'd failed them, just like she'd failed Danny.

Mikey and Lucy. Eight years old. Their lives snuffed out in a fingersnap.

What a bloody *waste*.

It wasn't just the people who'd died. It was the people around them who'd suffer. The teachers, who'd be blaming themselves for not keeping the kids under closer supervision. The parents, who'd be blaming themselves for working and not having the kids safely at home. The kids, who'd see those empty places in class and remember their classmates. The emergency services teams, who'd pushed themselves to the limits, but it still hadn't been far enough.

So many lives touched.

So many feelings up in flames.

Just like the school. Burned to a shell. And with nothing to prop them up…

'Brains.' Ray dropped into the seat next to hers and put his hand on her shoulder. 'You OK?'

'No. They…' She couldn't force the words out. 'The kids,' she rasped. 'Didn't…' She squeezed her eyelids tightly shut, willing the tears to stay back. 'Didn't make it,' she whispered.

Ray rubbed his hand over her back. 'Hey. You did your best. We all did.'

'Not enough.' She banged her fists hard on the table but she didn't feel the pain. She was numb from the heart out. 'It wasn't *enough*.'

'Nobody could have done more. Don't blame yourself. It was your first school fire, and you did well.'

'How the hell can you say that when they're *dead*?' she demanded. 'When I didn't rescue them? When I didn't do my bloody job!'

He exhaled sharply. 'I've been doing this a lot more years than you, but I remember the first kid I couldn't save.

I'll warn you now, it doesn't go away. And you'll always wonder if you could have done something differently. The next time it happens, you'll remember this—it'll bring it all back. It's just the way things are. We can't save everyone. We just do what we think's best at the time. It's all we *can* do.' He patted her shoulder. 'Really. I know you think you screwed up, but you didn't.'

'Yeah, right. Which is why you bawled me out.'

'I know I bawled you out.' He clapped her shoulder again. 'That's my job, because you didn't follow instructions and you put yourself at risk. And when you get to my position, you'll do exactly the same thing to *your* juniors when they break the rules.'

She shook her head. 'I'm not good enough to be station manager.'

He gave her a very pithy response. 'Tell me that in ten years' time. You'll do, Brains. You'll do *well*. You're on your way to being crew manager. A bit more experience and you'll be there. Just don't beat yourself up over this.'

How could she not? She'd been the one who'd failed to get the children out in time. The one who'd been there when the flames had shot through the room.

'Look, is Matt home?' Ray asked.

'Yeah.'

'Then go home. Make him take you out for a pizza or something. Anything to take your mind off it. Just as long as you're not on your own and you don't spend time brooding, OK?'

'Yes, guv.'

'I mean it, Kelsey. Like I said, we can't save everyone. We can only do our best—and that's what you did today.'

'Uh-huh.' She forced a smile to her face. But inside she felt sick. Angry with herself, because she should have done more. She should have got the kids out. And she hurt like hell on their parents' behalf. Just like she'd hurt for Danny. Still hurt for Danny and the ruins of his life. His job as a maths teacher gone. His place on the cricket team as demon bowler gone. His planned marriage to her gone. The rest of his life stuck in a wheelchair. Everything smashed up because one driver just hadn't been able to wait until he'd stopped driving before he'd made a phone call.

By the time Kelsey had driven home, she'd numbed the feelings. Damped everything down. Locked them in the little compartment where they belonged. And she was perfectly cool and calm when she walked through the front door.

Something smelt amazing, so she guessed that Matt was in the kitchen. Coping in his own way. He'd no doubt been chopping things viciously and stirring things and taking his feelings out on their dinner—when he'd had a rough day, he always headed straight for the kitchen.

She dropped her briefcase in the hall and went into the kitchen. 'Hi.'

'Hi.' He took the saucepan off the heat and enveloped her in a hug.

For a moment she allowed herself to lean into him. To let him support her. It would be so easy to bury her face in his shoulder and cry her heart out, knowing he'd be there to hold her and soothe her and make her feel better.

But she'd cried herself out years ago. She didn't do that sort of thing any more. She was Kelsey Watson, brainiac firefighter. Cool, calm and collected. She did everything logically. And having this much physical contact with her best friend was not a good idea. They were both overwrought. It would just take one tiny move from either of them and…

Images flashed through her mind of Matt's naked body twined with hers. Of his hands touching her intimately. Of his mouth tracking down over her abdomen. Of his—

Oh, no. This was way, way too dangerous. She stiffened and moved out of his embrace. 'You OK?' she asked.

'Yes. Well, no,' he admitted. 'So even if it hadn't been my turn to cook tonight, I would've made this.'

Funny how domesticity calmed him. It drove her bananas. Still, at least they'd never fight over the kitchen. And he was an excellent cook.

Actually, Matt was good at everything he did.

He'd be amazing at sex.

Ah, hell. She had to get her mind off that track. *Dinner*. 'Smells good,' she offered.

'Yeah, well, I thought your throat might still be a bit sore and pasta's easy to swallow.' He looked at her, and his eyes were very, very blue. 'Do you have any idea how much you scared me today?'

She shrugged his concern away. 'I was fine. It was a calculated risk.'

'Was it, hell! Mark told me how close you were. You ran out of oxygen, Kels. You could have—' His breath caught, as if he too was thinking of the two small bodies the fire crew had brought out of the flames.

She could have *died*.

Just like they had.

Again, she shrugged. 'Yeah, well. I know how hard it is to find a decent flatmate. I wouldn't put you to the trouble.' But she didn't meet his eyes. Couldn't. Not right now.

'Good. Don't you *ever* do anything like that to me again.' He paused. 'If you want to make yourself useful, you could make us a drink while I dish this up.'

Mmm. It would be all too easy to make a few Tequila

slammers and just let herself slide into oblivion. But that wasn't the way to deal with this. 'What do you want?'

'Whatever.'

So his heart wasn't in it either.

Without comment, she poured orange juice into two glasses and topped them up with sparkling water. Sat down while he brought two steaming plates over. And just toyed with the pasta because she couldn't bring herself to eat it.

'I'm sorry,' she whispered.

'Don't be.' He'd left most of his untouched, too.

'Tomorrow'll be better.'

'Yeah.' Though she didn't think he sounded that convinced either.

'I'm going to have a bath and an early night. I'm wiped.' She scraped the contents of their plates into the bin.

'Leave the rest of it. I'll do it,' he said. 'You've had a hell of a day.'

'So have you.' The kids had gone to hospital in his ambulance. He probably felt as guilty as she did that he hadn't been able to do more. Hadn't been able to save them.

'But I'm more used to this than you are,' he reminded her. 'Go and have your bath. It'll make you feel better.'

She wouldn't bet on that. Right now, she felt as if nothing would make her clean again. But she nodded and walked out of the kitchen.

'Kels?'

She paused at the doorway. 'Yes?'

'I'm here if you need to talk,' he said softly.

And she knew he didn't just mean talk. He meant she could cry all over him if she wanted to. That he'd hold her and make her feel safe. 'Thanks.' Though she wouldn't. Couldn't. Because, once she started crying, she didn't think she'd ever stop.

The bath didn't make her feel better. Didn't make her feel clean. She could still smell and taste the smoke. And the thriller she was halfway through didn't grab her either. She couldn't see the words on the page—just the leaping flames. The flames she hadn't been able to get past. The Japanese number-puzzle book she kept as a bedtime wind-down didn't help either. Her brain just refused to compute the calculations. The numbers ended up in the wrong place. So in the end she just dropped the book. Closed her eyes. And lay there in silence as the tears slowly leaked past her eyelashes.

It was stupid o'clock in the morning when Matt heard the scream. He opened his eyes to darkness. Had he really heard something, or had it been one of those peculiarly realistic dreams when you woke, convinced that something had happened—but it hadn't?

Then he heard it again. A high-pitched scream. Coming from Kelsey's room.

He jackknifed up, got out of bed and rapped on her door. 'Kels? You OK?'

Silence.

He opened the door just a crack. And then he heard her sobbing. Dry, tearing sobs, as if she was trying to hold them in and not wake him.

Ah, hell. He'd guessed how upset she was last night. He should've made her stay downstairs with him and talk it through, get all the pain out of her head. Now all he could think to do was give her a cuddle. Hold her close. Make her feel *protected*. Safe. No way could he just leave her to suffer and cry on her own. He wanted to make her feel better. Right now. He padded over to her bedside. 'Shove over,' he said.

''M OK,' she mumbled.

'No, you're not. And I can't just go away and leave you hurting like this. Not when I can do something about it.' He climbed into bed beside her and pulled her into his arms. 'I'm here,' he whispered. 'It's going to be all right.'

She shuddered and clung to him; her face against his chest was wet. He stroked her hair, just letting her cry it out.

Finally, she stopped shaking. 'Sorry,' she muttered. 'Bad dream.'

Yes, and he could guess just what it had been. Reliving the previous afternoon. The moment when the flames had burst through and put the kids out of her reach. And how he ached for her. He'd been there, too, felt the guilt at not being able to save someone. And it made you face your own mortality, too, made you vulnerable. Made you think about how it could have been you. A real but-for-the-grace-of-God moment.

'I'm here. It's going to be all right. You're not alone,' he said, and held her close.

'Matt. Stay with me tonight?' she asked, her voice decidedly wobbly.

He knew what she was asking for. A cuddle. A friend to hold her. She needed him, needed the comfort of another human being close by. And he'd be there for her. He'd take care of her, protect her from any hurt he could. 'I'm not going anywhere,' he told her, dropping a comforting kiss on her forehead. 'Shh. Go back to sleep.'

He lay on his back with her face pillowed on his chest and her arm curved round his waist, and listened as her breathing gradually slowed and deepened.

Weird. Although they'd given each other a back rub in the past, they'd never been this close before. Skin to skin. Because it seemed that Kelsey, like him, slept in the buff. He hadn't thought to put anything on—he'd just heard her scream and gone straight to her, knowing that she'd needed him. It had been an automatic response, wanting to be there for her and help her.

And now here they were in bed together. *Naked.* She'd asked him for comfort. Of course he'd said yes. He couldn't turn his back on her when she was hurting.

But he hated himself for being such a jerk. For thinking about—well, the fact that they were skin to skin. For thinking about sex. What Kelsey would claim was 'a typical guy thing'. And she'd be right. She was distraught—the last thing she needed was for him to leap on her like some Neanderthal.

Though there was more to the way he felt about Kelsey than just sex. A lot more.

Because now, lying here in the small hours with her asleep in his arms, he realised something. What he felt for Kelsey wasn't what he'd always thought it was. He liked her. He liked her a lot. They shared the same sense of humour, the same taste in films, the same taste in food. He enjoyed sharing a house with her. They had a close friendship. They understood each other's jobs.

But something had changed. He didn't know how or when or why, but it had changed. Yesterday, when he'd overheard Mark yelling at Kelsey over the radio and he'd realised she'd been in danger—real danger—his heart had almost stopped. If she died…

So he'd grabbed the radio and yelled at her himself. And when Mark had brought her out and pushed her through the window, Matt had been there to hold her. To carry her to safety. But most of all he'd needed to hold her, to know for himself that she was OK. It had been more than normal concern about a good friend. It had been sheer panic—because life without Kelsey would be unthinkable.

Somehow, she'd become the centre of his life.

Ah, hell. Matt had been in love before. He'd even been engaged. Lived with his fiancée. But what he'd felt for Cassie was like a pale imitation of what he felt for Kelsey Watson.

He loved Kelsey. Really, really loved her.

Thoughts of coming home to her were what got him through the rougher patches on his shift. And he got up in the morning smiling because he knew the first face he'd see would be hers.

But stupid o'clock in the morning wasn't the best time to try and work out this sort of thing. Particularly when she'd woken screaming from a nightmare, vulnerable and hurting. Sure, they needed to be honest with each other. But this was the wrong time for him to declare himself. For now, he'd hold her. Protect her from the world. Show her how he felt about her by his actions instead of pushing her with words.

And when the time was right he'd tell her how he really felt. Tell her he wanted to be more than her friend. Tell her just how much she meant to him.

That he loved her. Wanted to be with her. Wanted her to be his partner. For life.

CHAPTER FIVE

KELSEY woke at five o'clock the next morning—and nearly sat bolt upright when she realised she wasn't alone in bed.

Except she couldn't move. Because Matt was spooned against her, one thigh pushed between hers and his arm wrapped firmly round her waist, pulling her back against his body.

Uh. They couldn't have had sex. She would've remembered that…wouldn't she? So what the hell was he doing in bed with her?

She swallowed bile as the memories rolled back. The fire. Her bad dream. Screaming. Matt had stumbled into her room and held her. Let her cry it out. And she'd begged him to stay.

Oh, bad move.

This morning was going to be the mother of all awkwardness. Particularly as they were both stark naked. He was her friend—he'd felt obliged to stay with her when she'd asked. He was the kind of bloke who'd help anyone in a crisis. It was his job—but it was also who he was. Seven hundred years ago he'd have been riding a white charger and waving a sword, protecting those in his care:

nowadays, he had a big white van rather than a big white horse, but the principle was the same. Rescue and protect. That was what Matt did.

And when he woke up and discovered he was wrapped round her like this—like a lover—he was going to be extremely embarrassed.

Oh, great. How to ruin a good friendship in one easy lesson.

They'd never so much as kissed—not even when they'd been to a Christmas party together and drunk too much red wine. Matt had kissed her once under the mistletoe but it had been a chaste peck, nothing more. And they certainly hadn't fallen into bed together when they'd got home. If anything like that was going to happen between them, it would be on a night after a party when their inhibitions had been damped down by alcohol, surely?

Urgh. Her head felt as if she had a hangover, simply because she'd cried so much last night. What she wanted right now was a glass of freshly squeezed orange juice, followed by a milky coffee and a couple of paracetamol.

Well, what she *really* wanted right now was something that just wouldn't be sensible. Wriggling around in Matt's arms and kissing him awake would be the most stupid thing she'd ever done. Apart from the fact that he was due at the ambulance station in less than two hours, she knew that Matt simply didn't see her as a lover. He'd been badly hurt when Cassie had dumped him. He'd rarely dated since—he didn't want the hassle of a love life. Kelsey was with him all the way there. You fell in love, you got hurt. Been there, done that, and never again.

And if she was going to fall in love, it wouldn't be with her best friend. The one she wanted to keep for the rest of her life.

So now she had to work out how to wriggle out of Matt's arms without waking him. Then she'd find her clothes and have a shower, get dressed, grab some breakfast on the run and drive to the fire station. Her shift started two hours after his, but that didn't matter. She wanted to make sure she didn't see him until tonight—that would give him time to get over the embarrassment of waking up in her bed.

And then everything would be back to normal.

Sorted.

Matt woke, feeling muzzy-headed. Oh, hell. Don't say he'd forgotten to switch on his alarm and he was going to be late for work. Eyes still closed, he groped for the clock on his bedside table.

It wasn't there.

His bedside table wasn't there either.

Once that fact had hammered itself into his brain, he was wide awake. This wasn't his bed. It was Kelsey's. She'd gone to sleep in his arms last night, after crying a storm.

So where was she now?

He sat up, focused and grabbed her clock. A quarter to six. She didn't start until nine, so she couldn't have gone to the fire station yet. Maybe she was in the shower. Or downstairs having a cup of coffee. Or she'd taken their neighbour's dog for a very, very early walk.

Ah, hell. They needed to talk about this—he needed to know she was OK and he wanted her to know there wasn't a problem between them because of last night—but there simply wasn't time. He needed to get moving if he was to make his shift at seven. Why hadn't she woken him up? OK, so she might've felt guilty about interrupting his sleep last night, but she knew he was on the same shift as she was. Days. And that he needed to get up earlier than she did.

Unless…

Unless she hadn't been able to face him. Unless she'd been embarrassed by waking up in his arms—and neither of them had been wearing anything. So the chances were that when she'd woken up, they'd been snuggled together intimately.

And she'd chosen to leave rather than wake him.

In which case, he'd have to tread very carefully. The most important thing was that she was OK—that she wasn't still so distraught over yesterday that she'd done something stupid. Part of him knew that of course Kelsey wouldn't do anything drastic—she was way too calm and sensible for that—but this wasn't a normal situation.

It took him less than two minutes to discover that he was completely alone in the house. She hadn't left a note either. Which meant she was probably out with Alf's dog and had lost track of time. He scribbled her a note and left it on the kitchen table, propped against the potplant where she was bound to see it.

Hope you're feeling OK this morning. Sorry, couldn't wait for you, had to go on shift. See you tonight. M x.

It didn't say half of what he really wanted to say. But now wasn't the time for a big declaration, and in any case Kelsey wasn't one for making a fuss. A big romantic gesture—like a huge bunch of roses—would just fall flat.

So he'd cosset her in other ways. Give her a foot rub or a back massage. Cook her a decent meal. Make sure she didn't bury herself in her books and wear herself out. And when the time was right, they'd talk.

* * *

Kelsey was almost at the fire station when it happened. The flames came out of nowhere, flashing before her eyes. The heat. The roaring. Two terrified faces and the sound of a child's high-pitched screaming...

No. The high-pitched squeal of tyres, then the blast of a car horn. In her rear-view mirror she could see the driver of the other car gesticulating angrily and mouthing obscenities at her.

She shook herself and put her hand up in apology. He didn't look mollified, but at least he didn't carve her up at the roundabout. And he flashed his headlights at her in rebuke when she pulled into the fire station car park. Great. She'd given another driver a case of early morning road rage. Matt might have to deal with the consequences of that—and so might she.

She should've got a taxi in instead.

'You OK, Brains?' Mark asked when she walked into the mess room.

'Ish.' She wasn't going to admit to what had just happened. It had been an aberration—something that wouldn't normally happen. She'd been tired from her broken night, that was all. Tomorrow would be better. 'You?'

'Ish,' he said ruefully. 'I put the kids to bed last night, and Lia had to tell me not to hug them so hard.'

'Me, too,' Ray said. 'And I had to tell Finn about her friends.'

How did you do that? How did you explain to a child that her friends—children she'd played with and laughed with only that very day—had died and she wouldn't see them any more?

Kelsey shook herself. 'Rough. Is she OK?'

'Yeah.'

'What's happening with the school?'

'Safety officers said we might as well start the summer holidays a fortnight early.' Ray's jaw set. 'If they'd listened to me about those bloody sprinklers…'

'Maybe they will now,' Kelsey said softly.

Now that it was too late.

They were all thinking it, though none of them said it. It hurt too much.

Ah, hell. She'd coped with messy RTCs. Lorries, buses, a car smacking into a tram in the centre of Sheffield. She'd had to comfort people at the roadside, people who'd lost loved ones. She'd had to comfort people who'd watched all their memories, possessions that might not be worth a lot financially but meant the whole world to them, go up in flames. All times when she'd thought how easily it could have been her or someone she knew well. And she was trained to put the thoughts to the back of her mind and get on with making the area safe again. She'd been absolutely fine, even when there had been blood making the roads slippery and the smell of death in the air. She'd never had a problem with her job before. She hadn't even had a problem after the accident, because she'd been so focused on Danny and getting him to pull through the worst.

But this…this was different. The first time she'd lost a child in a fire. The first time she'd ever felt she'd let someone down, hadn't really done her job as a firefighter. The first time she'd *failed* someone, in her new life after the accident.

And it reminded her too much of the past. How she'd failed to get through to Danny. How she'd failed to help him when he'd needed her most. How she'd let him push her out of his life.

The morning dragged. The usual routine of checking the equipment, drills, two false alarms and a chip-pan fire that was out within ten minutes. The afternoon was even slower.

And then she had to go home and face Matt.

Maybe she could just pretend nothing had happened last night. After all, that note he'd left her had been pretty normal. Maybe her judgement was shot to pieces and she was worrying over nothing. She grabbed her mobile phone and texted him. *R u going out 2nite or shall I get takeaway 4 us?*

A minute or so later, her phone beeped. She flicked into the message screen. *T/way fine thanx.*

She didn't actually feel like eating anything, but she'd make the effort. Just as she had at lunchtime, when she'd choked down half a sandwich. She called in at the Chinese take-away on the way back, but froze in the doorway. The hissing of steam. The crackling sound of a stirfry. Like a whispered version of fire.

Again, flames shot across her vision. Two terrified faces. Mouths open in silent screams.

No. Not again. Please, not again, she begged silently.

'You all right, love?' one of the other customers asked.

'Yes. Thanks.' She shook herself, forced herself to walk up to the counter and ordered her meal. Luckily it was only a three-minute drive from home, and she managed that without incident.

Part of her wanted to tell Matt. Wanted him to hold her and comfort her again, as he had last night. But the better part of her didn't think it was a good idea. She was in enough of a mess with him already, without making it worse.

So she forced a smile on her face, did her usual balancing-briefcase-and-take-away-carrier trick, and closed the front door behind her with a swing of her hips.

'Hi. How was your day?' she asked brightly as she walked into the kitchen.

He looked up from the newspaper and his mug of tea. 'OK. Yours?'

'Yeah.'

She'd never felt awkward with him before. And she wasn't going to start now. She made an effort. 'I got crispy duck with pancakes.' His favourite. 'And bang bang chicken. And sesame prawn toasts.'

He grinned. 'It's just as well neither of us has a sedentary job.'

'How do you mean?'

'That's about a week's worth of calories you've got in that carrier bag.'

'No, it isn't.' Thank God, he was acting normally with her again.

'You're supposed to eat at least five portions of fruit and veg a day. There isn't even *one* portion in that lot.'

'I got chow mein as well,' she said, lifting her chin.

'I rest my case.'

She rolled her eyes. 'You can have a banana for pudding, if you're going to be fussy.'

'Yeah, while I watch you eat premium ice cream? I think not.'

She grinned. 'I'll make us banana splits.'

'Deal.' He stood up. 'What do you want to drink?'

'Water. I might not be as good as you are, Mr Perfect, when it comes to eating fruit and veg, but I do at least drink my eight glasses a day. Unlike some people, who drink way too much coffee,' she added pointedly.

He laughed. 'OK. So we both have a few bad habits.'

The dangerous moment was over. Everything was back to normal. Thank God. She let herself relax while they ate, but before she made the banana splits she propped her elbows on the table and rested her chin in her hands. 'Matt. About last night. I'm sorry I woke you.'

'No problem.'

'And…I appreciate what you did.'

'No problem,' he said again.

She noticed just how blue his eyes looked. Gorgeous. And that smile. Easy, relaxed. And it made her want to lean forward and kiss him. Gently. Tease his mouth with hers, until passion sparked between them and he kissed her hard. Then he'd pull her to the floor with him, take off her clothes while he kissed her, then kiss her again. All over. Teasing her with his lips and his tongue. Tasting her. Driving her over the edge.

Ah, hell. She had to get a grip. They were not going to have sex. 'It won't happen again,' she said quietly.

'Uh-huh.'

Please, let her phrase this bit right. 'And I don't want it to change things between us. We're still best friends, yes?'

'Sure.'

He sounded laid-back, but his expression didn't quite match his tone. Which meant that he wasn't at all comfortable with what had happened last night. She could have kicked herself. Why had she been so stupid? Why hadn't she just told him she was fine and let him go back to his own room? Why had she given in to the craving for comfort, the need to feel the warmth of his body against hers?

'Hey. I don't know about you, but I could do with getting out of here tonight. We're on nights tomorrow so we don't have to be up early. Want to forget the banana split and go clubbing?'

'Clubbing?'

'I just want to get out of my head. Not drunk,' she explained, 'just out of it. Dance it out of my system. Get hot and sweaty.' She wasn't going to let herself think about other ways of getting hot and sweaty. Like getting naked with Matt and crumpling their bedclothes. She was *not* going to wreck her relationship with her best friend.

'Clubbing it is, then.'

Was it her imagination, or had she just seen something in his eyes—something that said *he'd* thought about the naked option, too? No. Of course not. She really had to stop thinking about this morning and waking up in his arms— all warm and comfortable and *naked*. The feel of his thigh pushed between hers. The feel of his body curved round her.

'You can have the bathroom first, seeing as I've shirked washing-up duties all week.' She cleared the table and put the dishes on the drainer, ready to be washed. 'You've got twenty minutes to get dressed up.'

He scoffed. 'No way would you be ready in time. It takes you that long to put your make-up on.'

That was more like it. Teasing. Her best friend was back. She grinned. 'Don't exaggerate. We'll say thirty minutes, then. If I'm not downstairs, you can yell at me.'

'Deal.'

The moment that Matt saw Kelsey walk down the stairs, he regretted agreeing to go clubbing. She was wearing a little black dress that showed off her long, long legs, teamed with high heels. The problem was, he knew what lay underneath it. He knew from personal experience just how soft and warm and sweet-scented her skin was. And he wanted to peel her clothes off, very slowly. Kiss every inch of skin that he uncovered. Tease her with his mouth until her self-control splintered.

But how could he tell her he was crazy about her? How,

when she'd told him straight out that she didn't want last night to change anything between them? How could he be so bloody selfish when he knew that she was hurting? No, he had to put his feelings aside. Wait until everything was back on an even keel. Take the softly, softly approach.

They took a taxi into the city. Had a couple of drinks—beer for Matt, water for Kelsey. And then they headed for a club. Just what she needed. A loud, pulsing beat that would stop anything else going into her head. All she had to do was let the rhythm take over. Sway and let her body move to the beat.

It worked.

Until the DJ decided to mess about with strobe lights and dry ice. Too, too close to what she'd seen only the day before—smoke, flickering light, open mouths on the faces in front of her.

Except they hadn't been laughing: they'd been *screaming*.

She choked.

Matt was there by her side in a second, his arm around her shoulders, leading her off the dance floor to a quiet corner. 'OK. Deep breath in,' he said softly. 'And out. And in. And out.' He stayed with her until she was still and calm again.

'Sorry,' she whispered.

'What happened?'

'I'm OK. Just tired,' she lied. She couldn't tell him about the screaming in her head, the pictures that wouldn't go away.

'Want to go home?'

Yes. No. Right now, she had no escape. But at home she could crawl into bed and drag the covers over her head and try to shut it out. She shook herself. 'It was supposed to be a night out.'

'An early night's fine by me,' Matt said. 'Come on. Let's go find a taxi.'

They were one their way out when there was a yell. 'Help! Someone, help!'

Oh, God, please, don't let it be a fight. Please, don't let it be knives or smashed bottles, Kelsey thought. Men who'd drunk too much and slid from being happy to being nasty. Every time Matt was on nights on a Saturday, he had to deal with at least one drunken brawl. And she was always a bit on edge until she knew he was home safely. Though the same went for him: he'd admitted that whenever he heard of a huge fire, he was on pins until he knew that she was OK. Even though they both knew they were experienced emergency workers and good at their jobs, there was always that unnamed fear—because it only took a second for a situation to change dramatically, to shift from something they could deal with to something out of their control.

But they also each knew why the other needed to face the danger. Needed to do the job. Rescue people. Make things right again—as right as they could be, anyway.

'My mate's collapsed!' a girl yelled.

Matt looked questioningly at Kelsey. She nodded. Yeah, she needed to go home. But right now someone else needed him more.

Needed them more, she corrected mentally. She and Matt were a team. And they could do something, right here and now.

'What's happened?' Matt asked.

'My mate.' The girl didn't look more than about nineteen. 'We were dancing, and she...she just went down. She said she had a cramp in her leg. Then she collapsed.'

Without comment, Kelsey cleared a space round the girl to give Matt room to work.

Matt meanwhile loosened the girl's clothing, then checked her breathing and her pupils. 'She's not breathing,' he said to Kelsey. 'Pupils dilated.'

'You start mouth-to-mouth. I'll call the ambulance.' She grabbed her mobile phone from her bag and punched in the number for the emergency services. She gave her name, their location and brief details of the case, and asked for an ambulance.

'They're on their way,' she told Matt. She drew the girl's friend to one side. 'Has she taken anything?'

'No, no. Nothing like that. We don't do drugs.'

But the flicker of fear in the girl's face—plus the fact that the girl who'd collapsed had dilated pupils—told Kelsey otherwise. 'Look, if you're worried that we're the police and we're going to do you for it, you can stop worrying now. He's a paramedic and I'm a firefighter. Now, we need to know if she's taken anything because it'll help the ambulance crew—they'll know how to treat her. It's got nothing to do with the police. I promise.'

The girl bit her lip. 'She took Edward. We both did.'

Edward? Then Kelsey realised. Street name for Ecstasy, a stimulant drug that had a mild hallucinogenic effect. 'How long ago?'

'An hour.'

'Anything else?'

The girl shook her head. 'Just water. Well, I was drinking water.'

'Your friend?'

'She was busy dancing. Having a good time.'

Kelsey nodded. 'Chances are, she's overheated—you really need to take a break to let yourself cool down, and sip water while you're dancing.'

'Overheated?'

'It's not just feeling hot—sometimes you get cramps, or you feel sick or dizzy, or you get a major headache. You said she'd complained of cramp. Did you both take stuff from the same batch?'

'I think so.'

'Have you had any cramps, or are you feeling different at all?'

The girl shook her head. 'Just the usual. That rush that makes you feel on top of the world and makes everything look and sound sharp.' She smiled. 'You feel like everyone around you…well, they're happy.'

A feeling that didn't last. And it would be followed by a comedown that could last for up to half a week. 'OK.' Kelsey knelt down by Matt. 'She took E about an hour ago, hasn't been drinking anything—even water.'

'Mmm, and she complained of cramp just before she passed out,' Matt recalled.

'Should I get her some water?' the girl asked.

Matt shook her head. 'Better leave it for the ambo crew. If she drinks too much in one go, it could be worse than not drinking anything at all.'

'It's Saturday night. We were just having a good time,' the girl said.

Kelsey smiled grimly. 'I'll spare you the lecture, but there are better ways of getting out of your head.' Only, right now, for her it wasn't working. It was early days—it'd take a while to get over yesterday, she knew. But she was still beginning to wonder if the nightmare was ever going to die down.

'OK, she's breathing again,' Matt said. He put her into the recovery position and checked her pulse. 'Still a bit fast for my liking. Any chance of some wet towels to help cool her down?'

'I'll sort it.' Kelsey made her way over to the security staff. By the time she came back to Matt with the wet towels he'd asked for, the ambulance crew was already there. While Matt talked his colleagues through the handover, Kelsey drew the girl to one side. 'Best to go in with your friend. If you've taken the same stuff, and she's reacted to it rather than got overheated, you might have a similar reaction later.'

The girl shook her head. 'I'll get done for possession.'

'No, you won't. If you've got any on you, just flush it away. But don't risk your health. It's not worth it.' She took a deep breath. 'Trust me. Matt and I and the people we work with, we see it a lot. Too much. And the ones that could be avoided are the cases that really hurt. Go with them.'

Some of the pain in her heart must have got through to the girl because the teenager nodded. 'Yeah. All right. And…thanks.'

'No worries.'

Kelsey was shivering slightly as they left the club, and Matt slid his arm round her shoulders. 'Come on. You promised me a banana split.'

For a moment she thought about pulling away. Keeping the distance between them. But then she relented and slid her arm round his waist. It didn't mean anything. They were just friends. *Good* friends. 'Yeah. I think we're getting too old for clubbing.'

'Speak for yourself.' He grinned at her. 'Though you don't look so bad tonight.'

'Ah, you'll say anything for a banana split.' Gently, she removed her arm from his waist and slid out of his arms. Out of the danger area. 'Let's get that taxi, shall we?'

CHAPTER SIX

THE next two night shifts passed without event, then Kelsey and Matt had four days off. Normally they would have planned something. A trip out somewhere, maybe a long day out to the beach or a picnic and a hike in the Peak District. But she knew if she had another of these stupid flashbacks when he was with her, he'd nag her and nag her. Better to keep out of the way and say she was busy studying. And when she wasn't studying, she was doing puzzles. Focusing on the grids of a logic problem or wrestling her way through an alphacipher, where she had a list of words and the number of 'points' for each word, and worked out from that which number had been assigned to which letter of the alphabet.

When she'd exhausted her stock of puzzle books, she trawled the internet for more. Anything to keep her brain occupied and stop her remembering. Anything to make her brain so tired that she'd fall asleep the minute her head reached the pillow. Too tired to dream. Too tired to see the flames in her head, the screaming and the faces and the thick, choking smoke. And she'd keep going like this until she managed to bury the memories.

* * *

'Al, have you got a minute?' Matt asked, leaning against the doorjamb of the station manager's office.

'Sure. What's up?'

'Um…can this be confidential, please?'

'Of course.' Alan Brown gestured to the chair next to his desk, and Matt closed the door behind him.

'I've been reading about post-traumatic stress disorder.'

Alan frowned. 'Have you been having problems since the Bannington shout?'

'No, not me. And, as I said, I want to keep this confidential,' Matt said hastily. 'I'm asking about someone else.'

'Dale?'

'No, no one here. And I'd rather not say. It's just… there's someone I know I'm worried about. But I haven't actually come across a case of it before outside a textbook.'

'I've known a few,' Alan said. 'I was working in the London ambulance service at the time of the King's Cross fire—and a few of my colleagues were hit pretty badly after that. What do you need to know?'

'Just what I should be looking out for. And what I can do about it.'

'OK. First off, PTSD doesn't hit everyone who's survived a trauma—but it can hit you at any age. Sometimes it lies dormant for weeks, even years; sometimes it hits you straight away. It's triggered by something life-threatening that made you feel very afraid, helpless or distressed.'

Like the Bannington primary school fire. Kelsey hadn't been afraid for herself—but she'd been helpless to save the children. And she'd been distressed enough to have nightmares about it—nightmares Matt was sure she still had, even though she wasn't admitting to them.

'What are the usual symptoms?' Matt asked.

'There's a huge list of them. But in general you'll

expect someone who's suffering from PTSD to have sleep problems, nightmares, flashbacks they can't switch off. If they survived when others didn't, they might feel guilty. They might avoid anything that reminds them of what happened, or cut off from other people emotionally so they can just numb themselves against what happened. Or they might be on their guard all the time, irritable and jumpy.'

Kelsey was having nightmares, Matt was sure. And she was definitely avoiding things—and cutting herself off from others.

'So how's it diagnosed?'

'If they've been exposed to trauma, it's intrusive—they're still reliving it—they're avoiding things that remind them, they're hyperaware of their surroundings and it's really affecting their work or their social life, and it's been going on for a month, they meet the criteria.'

A month. So far it had been three weeks. 'Why a month?'

'The experts say it takes three or four weeks to come to terms with what happened and to understand it—it's an acute stress reaction, and it'll get better as you adjust to things. But if the reaction goes on for longer, then it's PTSD.'

Three weeks was 'normal', then. But he couldn't see any signs of it getting better. Matt sighed. 'OK. So if I know someone this is happening to…what can I do about it? I mean, what I read said you need to keep life as normal as possible, get back into routine, try relaxation exercises and spend time with family and friends. But if the person suffering this won't do it…'

'You need to get her to go and see her doctor,' Alan advised quietly.

Her. So Alan had obviously guessed who it was. Matt took a deep breath. 'Al, you'll keep this to yourself, won't you?'

'Of course. But if all the signs fit, she needs help.'

Matt nodded. 'From what I read, it's treatable by a mixture of psychotherapy and medication.'

'It's nothing to be ashamed of. And it's common. Firefighters are three times more likely to suffer it than anyone else.'

'I just have to get her to admit she needs help,' Matt said. And that was going to be the hardest part. Kelsey was more stubborn than anyone else he'd ever met.

'Do you want me to have a word?'

Matt shook his head. 'Better not, or she'll think I've betrayed her confidence.' Though he hadn't. He hadn't actually said her name or her occupation to Alan—his station manager had guessed. And Matt hadn't told anyone about the night she'd woken him with her screams and he'd climbed into bed with her to comfort her. That was just between the two of them.

'It might be worth having a word with her boss.' Alan looked sympathetically at him. 'You're caught between a rock and a hard place.'

'Yeah. Leave it, and I'm letting her down. Say something, and she'll take it badly.' To the point of maybe cutting him out of her life. He didn't want to risk that. But he didn't want to see her sink further and further into misery either. 'I'll work something out.' Somehow. 'Thanks, Al. I appreciate it.'

'No problem. Let me know if there's anything I can do.'

'Thanks. I will.' And maybe he'd talk to Kelsey's parents, see how she'd reacted after the car crash all those years before. It might even be that the Bannington fire had rekindled all the horrors from that time, too. His heart ached for Kelsey—and he wanted to make it all better. Kiss her better.

No. Now was *not* the time to push her into changing

their relationship. She needed to be better first. Meet him as an equal. No pressure. For now, he'd remain her friend. But the future…the future was something he'd hope for.

On the following Sunday morning—the last of their days off for that week—Matt rapped on the door of Kelsey's room.

'Come in.' She looked up from her computer. Matt had brought her a cup of tea. 'Oh, cheers. I could do with this.'

'Kels, we need to talk.'

Uh-oh. She didn't like the sound of this. Time to retreat. 'I'm studying,' she prevaricated.

'It's Sunday. You've been cooped up in here ever since you finished nights. You need a break.'

No, she didn't. She needed to keep busy. To keep her mind occupied and tire herself out so she couldn't think. 'I'm fine,' she lied.

'Come to the gym with me, then. Just for a break. It'll help you focus better.'

She shook her head. He sighed and sat on the edge of her bed. 'I knew you were going to do that.'

'What?'

'Make some excuse. You haven't been to the gym for over three weeks.'

She shrugged. 'So? I've been busy.'

'Not *that* busy. And you've always said the same as I have—that a good workout's the best post-shift stressbuster ever. But you haven't been to the gym since the day before the fire.'

He really wasn't going to let this drop, was he? Ice trickled down her spine. 'I'm all right.'

'No, you're not. You've spent the last three weeks avoiding going out.'

'Rubbish. We went clubbing, didn't we?'

'Once. And you had a panic attack. Had it not been for that girl collapsing…'

'I don't know what you're talking about.'

'Yes, you do. And it's not just that night. You ducked out of the last pizza night because you were studying. You made an excuse not to go to Izzy's party, when normally you'd be the first there and the last to leave. And you've been way too quiet these last few weeks.' Matt leaned over and took her hand. 'Kels, I'm worried about you.'

'No need.' She jerked her hand back. 'I'm absolutely fine.'

'Then come to the gym with me.'

'I'm not in the mood.'

'Are you avoiding me because we slept together and you're still embarrassed?'

She felt her face heat. 'No. We sorted that out. And anyway, it was sleep in the platonic sense, not having sex.'

'Yeah.'

Was it her imagination, or did he sound regretful that they hadn't made love?

No. She mustn't even *think* about what it would be like to wake up in Matt's arms after a night of making love. Because, once they'd done that, there was no going back. Their relationship would crash and burn. And she'd seen more than enough flames lately.

'So if you're not avoiding me, then you can't handle the gym because the place used to be a school.'

She folded her arms. 'Now you're being ridiculous.'

'Kels, this isn't like you. You work hard but you play hard, too. And you've stopped playing. You still take Floss for a walk every day—' Alf, their elderly next door neighbour, had had a bad fall two months ago and Kelsey had offered to exercise his dog Floss for him until he was up to walking at the dog's pace again '—but I bet your route's changed.'

To avoid the local junior school. How did he know? Had he been watching her? She shook herself. Now she was sounding paranoid. 'You're making a big deal out of nothing.'

'Then prove it to me.'

'How?'

'Come for a walk. We can go to Dovedale or something. And then we'll stop at a pub for a meal on the way home.'

A walk in Dovedale, in the Peak District, would do her good. Fresh air, hills and valleys and streams, and nothing whatsoever to remind her of the fire… And maybe he was right. Maybe she did need to get out of the house. Maybe in the open she wouldn't be scared to think. 'OK.'

'I'll give you ten minutes to turn your computer off and get your walking boots on.'

'No, I'll drive.'

He raised an eyebrow, but otherwise made no comment. 'OK. I'll sort out a backpack with water and some fruit.'

So he was planning a long walk, was he? 'Ten minutes.'

When she went downstairs, he was ready and waiting. She scooped up her walking boots, threw them into the back of the car with Matt's backpack and her waterproof— even in August, you couldn't guarantee it wouldn't rain.

'Where are you going, Kels?' he asked when she turned left instead of heading towards the Peak District.

'Dovedale.'

'You're going the wrong way, honey.'

'No, I'm taking the scenic route.'

She sneaked a quick glance at him and his expression told her everything. Damn. He knew her too well. He'd guessed exactly why she'd gone this way—to avoid driving through Bannington. Just like she'd avoided the gym. And he was bound to tackle her about it—probably when they were in the middle of Dovedale and she couldn't slam a door on him or walk away.

Why the hell had she agreed to come here with him? She must have been crazy. 'Which end?' she asked, as they crossed into Derbyshire.

'Ilam. I thought we'd head up to Alstonefield, down to Milldale and then past Dove Holes back down to Thorpe Cloud.'

Kelsey nodded. They'd done that walk before—the pretty route that circled the dale. 'Sure. But if you're thinking of the one that ends at the stepping stones on the river between Dovedale and Lindale, that's a four-hour walk. I hope you brought chocolate as well as fruit.'

'How did I know you'd say that?' he teased. 'Yeah, I brought chocolate.'

'Good.'

She parked, changed into her walking boots, and shoved her car keys into the pocket of her jeans. Matt shouldered into his backpack and let her set the pace as they headed across the fields towards Bunster Hill. She paused at the gap. 'Are we walking or climbing up?'

Matt nodded at the sky. 'Weather's good. Might as well make the most of the view.'

'Yeah.' And it felt good to be out here, in the middle of nowhere. Just the two of them and the sun and the wind and the steep ridge leading up to the top of the hill. Solid earth. Unlike shifting, moving, destructive fire.

They paused at the top to enjoy the view. She'd half expected Matt to tackle her there, but he waited until they'd passed the cottage after Ilam Tops and were looking down on Tissington Spires.

'So, are you still having the nightmares?' he asked.

Unwilling to lie directly, she just shrugged and said,

'I'm fine. I wonder why they call those towers of rocks Tissington Spires? They look more fins jutting out from the side of the valley.'

He completely ignored her attempt to change the subject. 'Kels, you're not fine. What happened in the fire…it'd give anyone nightmares. And of course it takes time to get over it. But— Look, you trust me, don't you?'

'Yeah.'

'Then I need you to do something for me. I need you to go and see your GP.'

She lifted her chin. 'I'm perfectly all right.'

'You're not. I think you've got PTSD—post-traumatic stress disorder.'

'No way.' She folded her arms. Did he really think she was the sort of person who'd start weeping and wailing at the first sign of danger? Someone who couldn't cope and ran away and left someone else to do her job? 'I'm not weak.'

He sighed. 'I *know* you're not weak. PTSD has nothing to do with weakness, Kels. It has everything to do with the fact that you're human. You've been through a truly horrible experience, and everything I've read—'

'Read?' she cut in.

'I'm worried about you. And I've heard of this kind of thing happening. So I looked it up.'

She felt the muscles in her jaw tighten. 'I see. And who have you discussed it with? Alan? Ray?'

He flushed. 'Give me credit. I've been trying to talk to *you* about it, but you're cutting me off. You're cutting everyone off.' He shook his head. 'And this isn't going the way I planned. I'm putting your back up and making a real mess of this.'

'Too right.'

'Kelsey. Look me in the eye.'

Unwillingly, she did so.

'I'm only nagging you because I—' He stopped abruptly, and her skin prickled with awareness. Because he…?

'Because I care. Because you're hurting. And because I'm your best friend and I want to make it better,' he said quietly. 'I can't stand by and watch you fall apart. Not when I can be there for you and do something to help.'

She willed the pricking tears to stay back. He cared. He'd noticed how she felt. He wanted to help.

But if she needed help, that made her weak. Dependent. Which was so *not* where she was coming from. 'I don't need to be made better. And I don't want to talk about it.'

'If you bottle things up, you'll feel bad.'

Ha. Been there, done that. And she didn't have nightmares about the accident and Danny. She'd bury the fire in the same way. 'I'm fine. Now, if you've finished, we have some walking to do.'

'I haven't finished. Look, I think you should go and see someone. Talk about it. There are things they can do to help you come to terms with it—it won't change what happened, but it can help you deal with it. Are you getting flashbacks?'

Yes. 'Just leave it, Matt,' she said through gritted teeth.

'Because, if you are,' he persisted, 'there's something called EMDR. It stands for eye movement desensitisation and reprocessing. It uses eye movements to help your brain process the flashbacks and deal with them.'

'I don't need to see a shrink or anybody else,' Kelsey informed him coolly. 'Now, we've got a descent to make. Let's go.' And she marched off along the edge of the woods, leaving Matt with no choice but to follow. She kept up a punishing pace during the rest of the four-hour walk, and when they got into the car she immediately turned the stereo up to a volume where Matt couldn't talk to her.

She was fine. She didn't need help from anyone or anything.

And the nightmares were going to go away. She'd will them to.

CHAPTER SEVEN

MONDAY was incredibly busy for Yellow Watch. Three false alarms—even though the crew were ninety-nine point nine per cent sure before they'd even left the station that the alarms were false, they couldn't risk not turning up to the calls. A call to help an elderly man get back into his house—he'd left the keys on the kitchen table and locked himself out. A car set on fire in a field of stubble—and because the car was reported stolen the crew had to stay until the police arrived. And the last call of Kelsey's shift was another RTC. It wasn't as bad as most of the ones she had attended, but it was her first case since the Bannington fire where the ambulance service had been called, too. It was at a particularly nasty crossroads—although it was officially a minor road, it was straight and flat and people drove way too fast down it. There was a crash there almost every week.

The police were already there when the fire crew arrived; most of the people in the accident were walking wounded.

'What's the situation?' Ray asked.

'The yellow car was turning right into the crossroads,' the policeman explained. 'Looks as if the driver thought he had enough space to get through but misjudged his distances, because the red car coming in the opposite direction smacked into the back of it. We've told the driver in the red car to stay where he is until the ambulance team arrives.'

Kelsey could see that the yellow car was still drivable and a man who was probably its driver was leaning against it, talking to one of the policeman. The other driver hadn't been so lucky. The impact had spun the car one hundred and eighty degrees, and smashed it into the front of another car that had obviously been waiting at the crossroads.

'OK, we'll make the area safe,' Ray said.

Kelsey knew the drill: check that the vehicles were all stable; there weren't any fuel leaks; and there weren't likely to be any explosions from pressurised suspension systems or air bag suspension units.

She was also expecting exactly what Ray said next. 'Brains, the ambo team aren't here yet. Once the red car's safe, can you have a look at the driver?'

'Sure, guv.'

A few minutes later, she was talking to the driver, assessing him for possible cervical or spinal injuries, when a hand squeezed her shoulder. 'Hey. Doing my job for me?'

'Yeah.' She smiled at the driver. 'This is Matt, one of the paramedics I work with. He'll get you out of here and check you over properly.' She straightened up and took a step back from the car so they'd be out of the driver's earshot. 'No loss of consciousness, no problems with breathing, no complaints of chest pain. Car's stable, doesn't look as if you'll need us to spread the car. But…'

'But?'

'He's complaining of neck pain. The police told him to stay put and try not to move. I was just about to get in the back seat and hold his neck in the neutral position until you lot got here.' The neck was the commonest site of spinal cord injury, simply because the neck was so mobile. Holding the neck still, in the 'neutral' position, stopped the head moving and prevented any additional cord or nerve-root damage.

Matt nodded. 'Cheers. If you could do that while I get a spinal board and the scoop stretcher?'

'Of course.' Kelsey opened the back seat of the car. 'Matt's going to get a spinal board and a stretcher. In the meantime, he's asked me to keep your neck as still as possible, to try and avoid any injury to your back and neck.'

'This what it takes to get a pretty girl's hands on you nowadays?' the driver asked ruefully.

She smiled. 'I'd hope not. It's pretty drastic!'

'My wife's going to kill me. She says I drive too fast. But it's this bloody road.'

'I know what you mean. We get called to this junction once a week, on average,' Kelsey said. 'It's a nasty one. And even putting the speed limit down along here hasn't made it any better. People still take stupid risks.' She paused. 'When Matt's put a collar on you, if you give me your wife's number we can get in touch with her for you, if you like.'

'Thanks, love.'

And then Matt was there with Dale and the spinal board.

'What I'm going to do now is put the collar on you to keep your neck straight,' Matt said. 'I'm going to tape it to your skin, just to keep it in place. It's going to feel a bit scary, but it shouldn't hurt. And if you feel any pain, anywhere at all, just tell me about it. That's what I'm here for.' Deftly, he slid the collar into place and taped it; Kelsey climbed out of the car to give Dale access and watched as they slid the spinal board into place and lifted the driver out.

She walked with them to the ambulance and, as promised, took the phone number to call the driver's wife. She was about to switch on her mobile phone to make the call when Matt climbed out of the back of the ambulance.

Matt noticed that Kelsey's face looked slightly pinched. Ah, hell. This was the first time they'd worked together since the school fire. It was probably bringing everything back to her. 'You OK?' he asked.

'Sure.'

She didn't look it. 'Have you said anything to Ray?' he asked gently.

'No need,' Kelsey said, her voice cool. 'And if you're going to nag—'

'You're going to lock yourself away studying technical firefighter stuff and not speak to me. I know.' He sighed. 'I wish you'd get it into your thick head that I'm only nagging because…' Because I love you. Because I want to take the pain away and make you feel better. Because I want to find a way to make you smile again. But, right now I don't know how. 'Because I care,' he finished.

'I know you do, and I appreciate it. But there's really no need. I'm perfectly OK.'

Subtext: she could look after herself and didn't appreciate being fussed over. Stubborn didn't even begin to describe her. He'd have to think up a different tactic. And, now he thought about it, maybe there was a way.

'See you tonight, then. It's my turn to cook, so we're having Moroccan chicken tagine and couscous and baby steamed veg.'

'Sounds good.'

He grinned. 'Excellent. I can butter you up with my culinary skills. And then I'll claim my favour.'

Her eyes narrowed. 'Favour? What favour?'

'Tell you later. I have a patient to get to hospital.'

'Matt! You can't just leave me dangling like this,' she protested.

'A *work* favour. And you'll have to wait to find out what.' He winked at her, and climbed behind the wheel of the ambulance.

Kelsey watched him drive away. A work favour? She knew that paramedics had to requalify every three years—maybe Matt wanted her to test him on some theory before his exams. He hadn't said anything to her about sitting exams, but what else could it be?

'You OK, Brains?' Ray asked when she went back over to the fire engine and helped to stow the gear away.

She nodded. 'Fine.'

'Remember I'm here if you need to discuss anything.'

She frowned. Matt had said he hadn't discussed anything with Ray... Or had he? He hadn't actually said the words 'No, I haven't said a word about PTSD to Ray', had he? But Matt wouldn't go to her boss behind her back. She was *sure* he wouldn't do something so underhand. 'There's nothing to discuss. Other than when I get all my competencies ticked off for the next level up, guv,' she said, striving for lightness.

Ray chuckled. 'They're in progress. But in answer to your next question, yes, if you keep on at your current rate I'll certainly put you in for interview for the next crew manager position we have in the area.'

'Good.' She smiled back at him. 'Everything's fine, guv.' And it was. She'd managed today without a flashback. Tomorrow would make two days. Then a week. Then a fortnight. Then a month.

Baby steps.

She'd make it.

And she didn't need anyone's help.

When Kelsey walked in that evening, she could already smell something fabulous simmering on the hob. She breathed in the scent. 'Cinnamon, coriander and ginger,' she announced.

'If you can tell what I'm cooking just from the smell, you obviously have a feel for it. So why do you hate cooking so much?' Matt asked.

'Because it's a waste of time, fiddling about with all that chopping and mixing and what have you, when the plate's going to be clean again in ten minutes' time.'

'So you'd rather I didn't do it?'

She held both hands up in a gesture of submission. 'Ah, no. It's relaxation therapy for you. I couldn't be so cruel as to deprive you of it.'

'Hmm.'

She walked over to the fridge. 'Want a drink?'

'A beer would go down very nicely.'

She dealt with the tops from two bottles and handed one to him. 'Cheers.'

'Cheers.' He lifted his bottle in salute and then took a swig.

'So what's this work favour?' she asked.

'Tell you after we've eaten.'

'Which is when?'

'Fifteen minutes.' He poured boiling water onto a bowl of couscous, then started to chop fresh coriander.

'So are you studying for exams?' she asked, not wanting to let it drop.

'Yes and no.'

She frowned. 'You're not thinking of a career change, are you? I mean, I thought you loved being a paramedic.'

'I do.'

'So *what*, then?'

He grinned. 'Aha. Got your curiosity piqued. You'll just have to be patient.'

She scowled. 'Just what are you up to?'

'All in good time. You can take your mind off it by laying the table.'

'Right.'

Irritatingly, Matt refused to be drawn even when they'd finished eating.

'Are you studying tonight?' he asked.

'Might be. So what's this favour?'

'It can wait until you've finished studying.'

'You're impossible,' she grumbled.

'I'll come and get you at half past nine. Go and do some work, woman.' He made shooing gestures with his hands.

She smiled, and headed up to her books. But five minutes after she sat down, the pictures started in her head. Two small, scared faces. Flames lashing in front of her, a barrier she just couldn't get through. The screams…

'No!' She thumped her fists on her desk. She was *not* going to let this happen. Deep breaths. Put the pictures in a compartment. Bury it where she'd never think of it again.

Ah, hell. And she'd been doing so well. Was this ever going to stop? Was Matt right? Did she need help?

She set her internet connection running and did a search for PTSD. She read through page after page, checking out the symptoms. No. It wasn't her. She was still doing her job to her full ability. Her social life was fine. This was just a normal reaction to a bad experience, and Matt was being paranoid. Making *her* paranoid, too—because here she was, trying to self-diagnose.

There was absolutely *nothing* wrong with her.

She switched out of the internet and forced herself to carry on with her studies. Though she jumped a mile when Matt rapped on her door and opened it.

'You OK?' he asked.

'Yeah. Just— You made me jump.' Because she'd been concentrating hard and had lost track of time. She wasn't being hypervigilant, or whatever that last article had called it. Jumpy. Irritable. And as for the headache that was developing—*that* was psychosomatic. She only thought she had a headache because she'd read that headaches were a symptom. She didn't have a headache *at all*. 'Is it half past nine already?'

'Yup.'

She leaned back in her chair. 'So what's this favour, then?'

'You need to go and have a shower.'

What? 'Why?'

'Because,' he said, 'it works better.'

He really was talking in riddles. 'What does?'

'Aromatherapy massage.'

She blinked. 'Let me get this right. You're doing something New Agey? Something flaky?'

He waved a dismissive hand. 'It's not *that* New Agey. And it isn't flaky, Miss Know-It-All. There have been studies on cancer patients that show aromatherapy's good for relaxation. And I've been thinking about my patients. Some of them, especially the older ones, really hate the idea of going to hospital. They're from a generation when going to hospital usually meant dying, and they think if they go into hospital they'll never come out again. It scares the hell out of them. So if I can do something to help them relax on the way in—like aromatherapy massage—maybe that'd be a good thing.'

Mmm, she could follow that. Logical. But… 'Why me?'

He curled his lip. 'Well, who else am I going to ask to be a guinea pig? Dale, Kirk or Alan?'

His colleagues or his boss? Mmm, he had a point. And Kirk in particular would use it as an excuse to tease Matt. Kirk the jerk, as she called him privately; apart from the fact she didn't like the way he treated Matt, she also didn't like the way he always tried to look down her shirt whenever they were out as a group. 'I suppose not.'

'If I ask one of the nurses, they'll think I'm trying to come on to them. I mean, if anyone else came up to you and asked, "Please, can I practise back massage on you?", what would you think? That he was trying to get into your knickers?'

'Er—yes.'

'Exactly. Which is why I need my best mate to do me a favour. If I ask you, you won't think I'm trying it on. So will you, please, go and have a shower, then wrap yourself in a towel and lie face down on the sofa for me? Oh, and I need the towel to be at waist level, so I get access to your upper back.'

From anyone else, that would definitely be a come-on—wanting her dressed only in a towel at waist level. From Matt…it was an extension of his work. He'd asked her to help, purely because she was his best friend. Which meant that what had happened the other night was forgotten, and he was safe again.

It was exactly what she'd wanted. So how come there was this tight little knot of disappointment in her stomach?

She had a shower and wrapped herself in a towel. When she got to the living-room doorway, she stopped dead. Matt had lit candles everywhere. Vanilla-scented tealights. And there was Mozart playing on the stereo.

'You can't do this in an ambulance,' she reminded him. 'Candles and oxygen cylinders really don't go together well.'

He rolled his eyes. 'Well, obviously. But we're not in an ambulance now, are we?'

'So this isn't a fair test. You're not doing it under the same conditions as you would in an ambulance.'

He grinned. 'Well, I could ring the station and see if they're on a shout. If they're not, we could always borrow a big white taxi for twenty minutes…'

She grinned back. 'Yeah, and you'd never hear the end of it.'

'Lie on the sofa and adjust your towel. I'll turn my back to preserve your modesty. And just rela-a-a-x,' Matt intoned.

She did as he asked. 'Ready.'

'Good. Close your eyes.'

She did, and felt a tiny pool of warmed oil on her back. 'Oh! I was expecting it to be cold.'

'Nope. Cold makes your patient tense up. It needs to be warm. Body heat, if possible.'

'So where did you get this stuff?'

'That new aromatherapy place in town. They made this up for me as a relaxation blend.'

Her suspicions rose. Had Matt done this just for her? Was this his way of trying to help her get over the post-traumatic stress disorder he thought she had but she knew she didn't have? 'What's in it?'

'Juniper, rose otto, cedarwood and sandalwood. And, before you ask, it's in a base of sweet almond oil.'

'And you honestly believe this stuff works?'

'You tell me when I've finished. Now, will you shut up? Put your head to one side. And breathe slowly and deeply—follow my lead.' He placed one hand on the base of her spine through the towel, and one on the back of her head.

'Matt, what are you—?' she began.

'Shh. This is what the book says I should do.' She heard the sound of pages rustling. 'Here we go. Breathe. In for four, out for four.'

Wow. This was powerful stuff, Matt thought. Heady. He wasn't sure if it was the scent of the oil or the candles. Or just the scent of Kelsey's skin. Maybe this had been a bad idea—a very bad idea. Because having his hands on her bare skin was sending all sorts of crazy messages to his brain.

He shook himself. Feathering, to start. Keeping his hands relaxed and his touch as light as a feather, he brushed his fingertips in long sweeping movements down her back.

'That tickles,' she murmured.

'Shh. It's meant to be soothing.'

'It *tickles*.'

OK. Stroke one was a failure. He turned the page. Next was effleurage. He placed his hands at the base of her spine, keeping his fingers close together but relaxed and pointing towards her head. Then he let his oiled hands glide up the strong muscles on either side of her spine, leaning into the stroke until he reached her neck. Then he let his hands fan across her shoulders and glide down again to her waist.

'Mmm. That's nice.'

Yeah. It was. All the way up—across—down. Though leaning into the stroke and pulling back again had ignited his libido. Slow and easy movements. Forward and back. Ah, hell. He'd known there'd be a risk that this would turn him on, but he hadn't expected it to be this fast, this hot. Forward and back. Slow and easy. Oh-h-h.

Just in time, he stopped himself bending forward to kiss the nape of her neck. He'd promised himself he wouldn't push her. Right now she was in a mess and she could do without the complication of a relationship. But he was going to make damned sure he was there when she was ready.

He forced himself to turn another page. 'Petrissage next.' God, he hoped she hadn't heard that husky note in his voice. Or guessed just how much he wanted her. He was careful to keep his lower body well away from her so she couldn't feel his physical reaction to touching her. 'It's a kneading action, which says here is meant to relax the muscles and aid circulation.'

'Kneading. Like bread?' Her voice was soft and slightly slurred. 'You make fabulous bread. Cinnamon rolls.'

'Hint taken. Next time we're on days off I'll make some for you.' He worked his way up the side of her body to her shoulders, alternately grasping and squeezing her flesh.

He *had* said it was a relaxation massage, hadn't he? Then again, he had a nasty feeling he'd told the aromatherapist it was for a woman. And maybe she'd jumped to conclusions and made it a blend that was sexy as well as relaxing. The only barrier between his fingertips and Kelsey's skin was a very, very thin layer of oil. Oil that let his hands glide over her. Touching her. Warming her muscles. Kneading out the tension.

Tension that had definitely transferred itself to him. He couldn't remember the last time he'd been this hard. And it would be so, so easy to dip his head and kiss the sensitive spot on her neck. Roll her over. Kiss her mouth. Touch her breasts.

'Friction,' he whispered.

And how he wanted the friction of his body sliding into hers. Right here, right now, in the candlelight.

Oh, this was good. She'd never had a massage before. Some of her friends swore by it, but Kelsey had never been one for beauty salons. Spending half an hour sitting in a chair while someone put goo on your face and wiped it off again was wasted time, in her view. Time she could spend doing something much more interesting.

But this—oh, this was bliss. Lovely warm, firm hands kneading her muscles and stroking her skin. Matt had changed position slightly so that he was working on the left side of her spine, his thumbs together, making tiny circular movements all the way up until he reached her neck. Deep, strong massage that was unravelling the tight knots in the muscles above her shoulder blades.

'Are you planning to give all your patients a back massage like this?' Her voice sounded slurred. She hoped he hadn't noticed.

'Neck, actually. And guinea pigs aren't supposed to talk.'

She made a sound that was meant to signify agreement but which sounded more like a purr of pleasure. Which it was, because he'd gone back to the gliding stroke again. Whatever it was called, it felt gorgeous.

But it also felt…sexy. Sensual. Supposing she hadn't been wearing the towel? Supposing she rolled onto her back and the towel just fell away?

No. Absolutely not. Right now she couldn't trust her feelings. Matt was her best friend. She'd already made things difficult between them by asking him to stay with her while she'd slept that night. This massage was just his way of showing her that things were back to normal and they were still friends. Good friends. But *just* friends.

'I need you to change position now,' Matt said.

His voice sounded odd. Husky. As if he was purring. Change position. Was he going to ask her to roll over? Was he going to lean down and kiss her, let his fingers work even more magic as they touched her more intimately? Had the way he was touching her affected him the same way it had affected her?

'I want to do your neck now. Lift your head up slightly, put one hand on top of the other and rest your forehead on your hands,' Matt said.

That'd be a no, then. He wasn't planning to make this anything more than just a practice. Which was sensible. And she really should follow his lead. Leaping on him might make her feel good for a night, but then she'd have to pay for the pleasure. Pay a price she just wasn't prepared to pay. Ruin everything.

So she did what he asked, relaxing herself and letting him move her arms to a slightly more comfortable position. He kneaded the muscles in her neck, up and down, and the tension began to drain from her again.

'Relax your hands and put your head to one side again,' Matt directed.

He kneaded her shoulders, working out the tension, then went back to the lovely long gliding strokes. By the time his touch had lightened to featherweight again, she was almost asleep.

'Breathe deeply,' Matt whispered, placing one hand on her spine and the other on her head. 'Breathe with me. In for four, out for four. Deep. Even.'

She did. And when his hands finally left her skin, she felt…lost. Wanted them back. Except now she was, oh, so drowsy.

'How do you feel?' he asked.

'Wonderful. Though I can't keep my eyes open. I think I'm going to bed.' It would have been better if she'd been going to bed with *him*—but that really wasn't a good idea.

'Sure. See you in the morning.'

'Yeah. And, Matt?'

'Yes?'

Was it her imagination, or did he sound hopeful? No. It was her imagination. Wanting something she couldn't have. 'Thanks.' She gathered the towel round herself and stood up. 'Do this to your difficult patients, and they'll be like lambs when they get to the emergency department. You'll be able to do anything you like with them.'

'Anything?'

No, she was just dreaming that wistful note in his voice. He'd made it perfectly clear that they were just friends. She stood on tiptoe and kissed his cheek. 'You're a good man, Matt Fraser. The best.'

And then, before she made a fool of herself and begged him to go with her, she walked out of the room.

CHAPTER EIGHT

To KELSEY's relief, Tuesday was just another day—but Wednesday's night shift was a lot tougher.

'Turnout, vehicles 5 and 57. Alarm raised at Sotherton Road Sixth Form College.'

Oh, God. The local sixth form college. *A school.*

It was in the middle of the school summer holidays, but she knew that the college ran night-school classes. And not all the classes were exam-based or just run during term-time. The keep-fit and dance classes continued through the summer, and there were small one-off courses as well. Photography, art, computing...

Kelsey fought a wave of nausea and grabbed the call sheet from the fax machine before pulling on her boots and firefighting gear. The seat at the back of the fire engine looked a long, long way up, and the muscles in her arms felt as if they'd suddenly lost all their strength.

Get *in*, Kelsey. You're needed, she told herself harshly. This wasn't the time for nerves. She had a job to do and she was holding everyone up by dithering. She really had to pull herself together.

'No more details, guv,' she said as she handed the sheet to Ray and strapped herself into her seat.

He looked up from the computer. 'Nothing more here either. Well, let's see what we've got when we get there. Luckily we're close.'

'You OK, Brains?' Paul asked. 'You look a bit white.'

'Fine. Just a bit tired. Went hiking with Matt at Dovedale over the weekend,' she prevaricated.

Paul nodded, as if accepting her explanation, but he still looked faintly worried about her.

Hell, hell, hell. The last thing she wanted was to let anyone down on the team. She just had to get control of the pictures in her head. Lock them away. Not think about those two pinched little faces. Not hear the screams.

Joe pulled up in the quad of the college five minutes later, and they climbed out of the engine. No sign of smoke, no smell of burning. But they couldn't take any risks. They'd just got most of the kit off the engine, ready to deal with an incident in progress, when a security guard came up to them.

He looked decidedly sheepish. 'Sorry, mate. We were, um, testing the fire alarm. Forgot to tell the monitoring company.'

'OK.' Ray looked at the crew and rolled his eyes. 'Time to pack up.'

'I'm sorry I wasted your time,' the security guard said. 'Soon as I realised, I started to ring through, but you were already here.'

Ray nodded. 'I'll check the alarm system's reset properly.'

Kelsey concentrated on getting the equipment back into the engine. False alarm. No fire. Nobody hurt. Nobody dead.

So why was it that every time she blinked, flames seemed to roar across her eyeballs?

'Are you sure you're OK?' Mark asked.

'Fine.' She regretted the sharpness of her tone the second she saw the hurt in his face. 'Look, I'm just a bit tired.'

'Put it down as a FADA,' Ray said when he climbed back into the fire engine. False alarm due to apparatus. 'Let's just hope that it's a quiet shift.'

There was a weekly maintenance routine: Mondays meant the weekly tests on all the equipment, Tuesdays meant cleaning the first appliance and testing the second, Wednesdays was usually training, Thursdays meant cleaning the second appliance and testing the first, and Fridays were catch-up nights when they completed any tasks they'd had to leave on the previous four nights due to callouts.

'What's the training for today, guv?' Joe asked.

'Hazchem,' Ray said. They didn't deal with that many spillages of hazardous chemicals, but they needed to keep up to date with the best way of dealing with them and keeping workers from the other emergency services safe, too.

Kelsey let the conversation wash over her on the way back to the fire station. Somehow she managed to get through the rest of the night and the whole of the next week—but the following Tuesday night there was a call to one of the city tower blocks.

'Someone stuck in a lift?' Mark raised an eyebrow as he climbed into the back of the fire engine. 'You sure? Have they called the maintenance company?'

'Yes. They can't get anyone out for at least four hours,' Ray explained.

'On a hot, sticky day like today, that's not going to be a pleasant wait,' Mark said with a grimace. 'So the lift company's actually being nice for once and we're going to do their job for them?'

'They don't have a choice,' Ray said. 'Normally, they'd have told us they'd deal with it.' Because the fire brigade charged the lift maintenance company to open jammed lifts—which usually failed in the first place because they hadn't been maintained properly—and because of the potential damage caused to the lift mechanism, lift companies tended to wait for their own technicians to deal with it. 'But there's a child stuck. A child with asthma. The ambulance is on its way.'

A trapped child.

'How old?' Kelsey asked, trying to sound as cool as possible.

Ray checked the screen. 'Eight. There's an older child with him—his sister. She's the one who called in.'

Eight years old. Same as Mikey and Lucy. A little boy.

And he had asthma. Matt had told her about asthma cases before now. It was a condition where the child's airways were inflamed and responded rapidly and strongly to stimuli, so the child wheezed and coughed; the airways narrowed so much that the child couldn't breathe out properly. The child then panicked and the situation started to spiral.

She also knew from Matt that asthma could kill. She remembered what Matt referred to as a 'silent chest', where the wheezing stopped. It was far more dangerous than wheezing, because it meant the patient wasn't moving enough air through their lungs to create a wheeze.

Oh, God. She didn't think she could handle another case with a child. Not now. Not when the Bannington fire was still so raw in her head.

But she didn't have a choice. When you worked for the fire and rescue service, you couldn't just pick which calls you wanted to respond to. You had to take everything that came your way.

'The lift's stuck between floors two and three,' Ray said. 'Kelsey, Paul, come up with me to floor two—we'll

try to do what we can from there. Mark, I want you to go
down to the lift control motor room with radio comms. Joe,
stay with the vehicle.'

'Right, guv,' they chorused.

Ray tapped on the lift doors when they arrived at the
second floor. 'Hello? It's the fire crew. Can you hear me
in there?'

'Yes,' a muffled voice called back.

'Is that Courtney?'

'Yes.' Muffled, with an edge of fear.

'I'm Ray, one of the firefighters. We're going to get you
out of there. What we're going to do is check the lift, then
we'll wind you up or down, depending where the lift is,
open the doors and get you out. How's your brother?'

'Scared. Wheezing. Can't talk much.'

'It's OK. Hang on in there. We're going to get you out
very soon, love,' Ray called. 'And an ambulance is on its
way to look after your brother.'

Kelsey sincerely hoped the paramedic would be Matt. He
was brilliant with children. Brilliant with patients, full stop.

'You might hear a few noises, but don't be scared. We're
here, and we're not leaving until we've got you both out
safely, OK?' Ray said. 'What's your brother's name?'

'Noel,' Courtney said.

'Guv, I'm in the control room. Over,' Mark said through
the radio.

'Mark, I want you to isolate the power to the lift and
check the pressure gauge attached to the lift pump. Over.'

Standard procedure, Kelsey thought. Ray needed to
assess the situation to work out how to deal with it. If the
pressure gauge was zero, that meant that the car was held
in place either by the emergency braking mechanism or by
an obstruction in the lift shaft, so it would be too danger-

ous to move anyone until the lift engineer got there. They could secure it with ropes, but that would put the firefighters at high risk—they could fall into the lift shaft or be injured if the lift moved. Plus the lift might be too heavy for the fire service lines; the knot would be the weak point and could give way under a shock load.

The radio crackled. 'There's a pressure reading, guv. Over.'

Good news: it meant they'd be able to work with the lift. Move it themselves.

'Use the hand pump to move the lift upwards. Over,' Ray said.

If the lift moved up, it meant the weight of the lift car was being held by the suspension mechanism and it was safe to start lowering the lift through the emergency lowering valve. But using the hand pump was a very slow process—the lift would only move a couple of millimetres for every stroke of the pump.

'Courtney, you might feel the lift start to move upwards a little bit. Don't worry—we're doing it,' Ray called. 'You're not going to fall.'

'It's moving, guv,' Kelsey reported.

'Good.' He cleared his throat. 'Courtney, what we're going to do now is lower the lift so we can get you out.'

It was always best to open the doors at the ground floor; otherwise there was the risk of a 'shear trap'. If the doors were open at a higher level, someone could be reaching through the gap and if the lift car fell, it would trap that person between the top of the lift car and the floor of the opening. Or worse than trapping, the closing of the gap could act like a guillotine. It was a risk no officer in charge would want the fire crew to take.

'It's going to be very slow and gentle,' Ray continued. Lowering the lift through the emergency valve meant draining hydraulic oil from the system and letting the lift car descend slowly by the force of gravity.

Ray switched back to the radio. 'Mark, operate the emergency lowering valve for two seconds, then stop.'

'It's definitely moving, guv,' Kelsey said.

'Good. OK, Mark, keep it going.' Ray raised his voice. 'Courtney, we're getting you down. Nice and slowly. OK?'

'OK.' But the young girl's voice wobbled slightly.

Hardly surprising, Kelsey thought. She was trapped in a lift. A small, stifling box. Just as Mikey and Lucy had been trapped in that cupboard…

Oh, God. She closed her eyes and she could still see the sheets of flame ripping across the room. The fear in the children's eyes. The knowledge in those little faces that she wasn't going to be able to save them.

Hell. She had to get a grip. This wasn't the same thing at all. A boy and a girl, yes, but they weren't the same age. This was a lift and not a cupboard, and the crew hadn't been called to deal with a fire. *Shut up and do your job*, she warned herself.

'Hey. The air's a bit thin up here,' a deep voice said.

Kelsey recognised Matt's voice immediately. Suddenly everything seemed a lot better. A lot *safer*. Crazy. She was the one who was supposed to make the area safe—Matt dealt with the medical side of things. But she was very glad he was there. 'Hey, Matt.' She strove to keep her voice light. 'How's it going?'

She quickly brought him up to speed.

He nodded. 'OK. I'll introduce myself.' His voice dropped to a whisper. 'But before I do… Are you OK?'

'I'm fine.' Not quite true—but his presence definitely calmed her.

'Hello, Courtney—I'm Matt, the paramedic,' he called. 'Can you hear me OK?'

'Yes.'

'How's your brother doing?'

'He's wheezing a lot. He's got asthma, 'cept Mum won't let him have his inhaler. She stays steroids are what bodybuilders use and he should have herbal stuff instead.'

Matt cursed softly. 'Courtney, it's not the same sort of steroid, love. It's stuff that your body produces naturally.'

'I know,' Courtney yelled back. 'I looked it up on the internet. I told her. But she doesn't believe in drugs. Except pot.'

'I know the type,' Matt muttered to Kelsey, rolling his eyes. Then he raised his voice again so Courtney could hear him. 'OK, love. We'll sort him out as soon as you're out of there. Are you all right?'

'I'm a bit scared,' she admitted. ''Cos of Noel.'

'No need to be scared, because I'm here and I've got medicine to help him breathe,' Matt called. 'Try and get Noel to calm down. I know it's scary when you've got asthma—it's like trying to breathe out through a drinking straw. But try and get him to take long, slow breaths if you can. Does he like music?'

'Ye-es.'

'Can you sing him a song?'

'What sort of song?'

'Any song. Hey, tell you what. I've got a firefighter with me and she's really, really good at singing. You tell her a song Noel likes, and she'll sing it to you.'

Kelsey's jaw dropped. 'You want me to *sing*?' she hissed.

'Anything to get the lad calmed down.' He winked at her. 'Go for it. You'll have to improvise with the hairbrush.'

'Hairbrush?' Paul chuckled. 'Oh, this is priceless. What I would give to have a video camera.'

Kelsey pulled a face at him.

'I'm tone deaf. Matt, does she really sing at home in front of a mirror with a hairbrush?'

'That,' Matt said with a wink, 'would be telling.'

'Oh, shut up, you two. Join in with me, Courtney,' Kelsey called, and started to sing.

They were halfway through a song when Courtney stopped singing.

'What's wrong, love?' Ray called.

'Noel's wheezing ever such a lot. Last time he was like this, he turned blue and we had to call the ambulance.'

Matt cursed. 'How long's it going to be before the lift's down, Ray? It sounds as if he's got severe asthma. It could turn life-threatening at any second. If he stops wheezing it could be fatal. We need him out fast.'

'The lift's going down by gravity. How fast do you need him out?'

'Now, preferably,' Matt said.

Ray nodded and radioed down to the lift control room. 'Mark, we need to get them out now. Stop the valve. Over.'

'Stopping the valve, guv. Over,' Mark responded.

'I'll go in,' Kelsey said.

Ray shook his head. 'Until we're at ground level, there's still a shear trap risk. If the lift moves when you're halfway into the car… No. I'm the senior officer here. I'll do it.'

'But I'm lighter than you,' Kelsey said. 'I'm the lightest here. Which means there's less of a risk if I go in the lift.' She took a deep breath. 'Guv, I need to do this.' To save a child—it wouldn't bring Mikey or Lucy back, but it would make her feel better. Make her feel that she'd done her job this time, not failed.

Matt laid his hand on Ray's shoulder. 'She's right, mate. She's the best one for this job.'

Ray nodded and radioed down to Mark. 'Apply the brake. Over.'

'Done, guv. Over.'

Paul and Ray forced the inner and outer doors open. The floor of the lift was still three feet above the floor of the corridor.

'You sure about this?' Ray asked.

No. Nausea roiled in Kelsey's stomach, and her muscles felt more like useless blobs of jelly than anything else. But she was bloody well going to do this. She wasn't going to let the fear beat her. She didn't quite trust her voice, so she just nodded and hauled herself up into the lift. Crossed the shear trap.

'It's OK, we'll get you out of here.'

That was what she'd said last time—well, almost. Except this time there was a difference. She really *was* going to get these kids out. The lift was secure and the brake was on and the car wasn't about to plummet downwards and snap them in half as they climbed out of the lift.

No smile from either child, though she could see why. Noel was too weak and Courtney was too scared.

'I'm going to lift you out to the paramedic, Noel,' Kelsey said, 'and then I'm going to help you down, Courtney. Everything's going to be fine now.' Gently, she lifted Noel. Matt was already waiting with open arms for the little boy.

She turned back to Courtney and gave her a hug. 'Hey. You were super-brave in here. Braver than I would've been.'

Braver than she still was. Like a coward, she was shaking inside.

'Let's get you out of here. You can go in the ambulance with Noel, if you like. Do you want us to call your mum for you?'

Courtney shook her head. 'No point. She's out with her boyfriend.'

And Courtney was—how old? Ten? Twelve? 'What about your babysitter? She must be worried.'

Again, Courtney shook her head. 'No babysitter.'

Kelsey damped down her anger. Now wasn't the time. But the children's mother definitely needed a rocket up her backside, in Kelsey's view. Sure, of course she deserved to have a life of her own—but she had kids. Kids who were too young to fend for themselves and needed her to put their welfare first.

Matt was already checking Noel over when Kelsey helped Courtney down from the lift.

'How is he?' Kelsey asked.

'Tachycardic, tachypnoeic,' Matt murmured, using jargon that he knew the fire crew would understand but which wouldn't scare the little boy's sister. Noel's pulse was too high, over a hundred and twenty beats a minute, and his breathing was too fast, at over thirty breaths a minute. He was too breathless to finish a sentence in one breath—and when Matt palpated the boy's neck muscles he could feel that Noel was using the muscles of his neck to help him breathe.

Not good.

Though it could be worse. If Noel's airways swelled up much more, they'd obstruct his breathing. The awful-sounding wheezing would stop—but it would be a far, far more serious situation.

'OK, Noel. I know if feels as if you're going to die, but I promise you you're not. What I'm going to do is give you something special to breathe in—it's called salbutamol, and it will help relax your airways and make it easier to breathe.' Deftly, he administered 4 mg of the bronchodilator drug. 'Breathe in for me. Nice and slow. That's it. In—out—and another, in—out. Good boy.'

A quick check of Noel's oxygen saturation levels showed Matt that they were too low. A reading of 90 breathing room air wasn't good enough. 'I'm going to put a mask on you now—it'll give you some oxygen and you'll start to feel better.' He put the mask on the child and started running the oxygen through at six litres a minute.

'Courtney, love, has this happened before?' Matt asked.

Courtney nodded.

'Often?'

She stared at the floor, clearly not wanting to betray her mum.

'It's OK, you're not going to get into trouble,' Matt said, his voice gentle. 'It'll just help me treat him properly, that's all.'

'Fourth time in six months,' Courtney said, her voice the tiniest whisper.

'Uh-huh.' Matt already knew from what she'd said earlier that Courtney's mother didn't give the boy his inhaler. 'Did the doctors at the hospital say anything last time?'

She nodded. 'Mum had a fight with them. She discharged him and took him home.'

Matt's glance met Kelsey's. She looked positively murderous. And, yeah, he could understand that. He felt that way himself. Ignorance and prejudice were two of the more difficult battles to win. 'I'm going to take Noel to hospital now,' he told Courtney. The guidelines said that if the asthma was severe rather than life-threatening, it should be treated for twenty minutes before the patient was admitted to hospital. But Matt was going to override that. There was a child involved, Noel had had previous severe attacks and it was evening—which meant there was a chance he could have another attack later in the night. Given his mother's views, Noel wouldn't get the doses of the beta-2 agonist drugs he needed. He'd be better off in the emergency department and then moved up to Paediatrics.

And Matt was going to brief the ED team about the parental situation, as well as suggesting that they contact the GP and Social Services.

'Is he going to be OK?' Courtney asked.

Clearly the grimness of his thoughts had shown in his face, Matt thought. 'There's a good chance he'll be fine,' he reassured the girl. 'But Noel needs treatment.'

She bit her lip. 'Is my mum going to get into trouble?'

Courtney's mother certainly wasn't going to get an easy time of it, but Matt kept that to himself. 'Someone will explain to her about how asthma works and exactly why Noel needs his medication,' Matt said. 'Help her understand that if she doesn't give him his medication properly, she's making his life much harder.' Not to mention putting it at risk. 'Come on. You can ride in the back with me and Noel.' He glanced at Kelsey and mouthed, 'You OK?'

She nodded, though he noticed that she didn't meet his eyes. Ah, hell. She was remembering Mikey and Lucy. He was, too. That had been the last time he'd taken a child into the ambulance... And the child hadn't come home again.

Unless he and Dale were called straight out on another shout, he'd stick around the hospital for a bit until he was sure that Noel was stable, then he'd text Kelsey some reassurance.

* * *

'Time to secure the doors,' Ray said. 'The last thing we want is a bunch of teenagers playing chicken and falling down the lift shaft.'

When they'd finished securing the doors, he radioed down to Mark. 'Usual notice on the power unit, please. Over.'

'Already done,' Mark said. 'Over.'

The notice was standard: it warned security staff that emergency isolation of the power had taken place and told them explicitly not to reinstate power until checks had been completed by a qualified lift engineer.

When they got back to the station, Kelsey checked her mobile phone while the rest of the team went for a teabreak. There was a text from Matt: *Kid stable, in 4 obs only cos of social circs. Will pull through, no probs.*

She sagged in relief. *Ta 4 telling me*, she texted back.

'Brains, can I have a word?' Ray asked when she walked back into the mess room.

'Sure, guv. Oh, Matt's just texted me. The boy's going to pull through.'

'That's good to know,' Mark said, smiling at her.

Ray manoeuvred her through to his office. 'Sit down.'

Then it hit her. Ray wanted a word in his office. In private. She sat down and folded her hands on her lap, hoping that she looked calmer than she felt. She didn't think she'd done anything wrong at the lift rescue. But Ray looked worried. Which meant trouble. 'What's up, guv?'

'Are you sure you're OK?' he asked.

Kelsey tried to laugh it off. 'Course I am.'

He raised an eyebrow. 'So what was all that about at the tower block?'

'I…' She shook her head. 'Nothing.'

'It wasn't nothing. You were so adamant that you were going to be the one to do the rescue. Kelsey, if you're still being affected by the Bannington case, you need help. Nobody's going to think less of you.'

Oh, yes, they were. *She* thought less of herself, for one. 'I'm fine,' she insisted.

'OK. But bear one thing in mind. If you're *not* OK and you turn up for duty, you could be putting the rest of the crew at risk,' he warned.

'I wouldn't do that,' she said. Though she knew deep down that he was right. If she had a flashback while fighting a fire, she could put herself and her crewmates at risk of injury, even death.

'I know you wouldn't—not intentionally. But sometimes it's hard to shake off a case. It's always bad when kids are involved. I've seen firefighters go under before and I'll see it happen again,' Ray said, his voice very gentle. 'If you need help, you've got my backing. Just think about it.'

'Sure, guv,' she said.

But there was nothing to think about. If she couldn't be a firefighter any more…what was left?

CHAPTER NINE

WHAT was that?

Matt struggled to pull himself out of sleep. He'd heard a noise. Or had he been dreaming? The house was silent now. He strained to hear. Nothing. Maybe it had just been his imagination.

Or maybe Kelsey had woken with yet another nightmare and was crying into her pillow, trying not to wake him.

He climbed out of bed and padded over to Kelsey's door. He listened in the doorway. Nothing. Must've been a dream, then.

Just as he turned to go back to his own bed, he heard a muffled sob.

Ah, hell. He knew he should keep some distance between them—but how could he leave her to deal with this on her own? Even though she wasn't admitting it, she was suffering. She needed help. She needed *him*.

Quietly, he rapped on the door. Walked in. Sat on the edge of her bed. 'Kels?' He stroked her hair. 'It's OK. Just a bad dream.'

'I couldn't save them, Matt. I *failed*.'

'It wasn't your fault. Nobody expected the fire to suddenly come shooting out like that. None of the rest of the crew could have done more,' he reminded her. 'And look at earlier. You made a difference. If it wasn't for you, Noel could have been in a really bad way. You got him out while we could still help him. Before he turned critical.'

'It's still not enough. It doesn't make up for Mikey and Lucy.'

Her voice sounded gravelly—had she cried herself to sleep before she'd woken from her nightmare?

'We can't save everyone, Kels. I have heartbreak cases, too. Cases where the patients arrest on me and I can't get them back. Cases where I think if I'd had just ten more minutes, I could have saved them. Sometimes it's just not meant to be.'

'But they were only kids! They were eight years old. It's…' The rest of her sentence was choked off.

'Hey.' He shifted to pull the duvet aside and slid into the bed beside her. 'Come here.' He pulled her into his arms, pillowing her head against his chest. She was shaking. Still crying? He wasn't sure, though her face was damp. He held her close, stroking her hair and soothing her. 'It's going to be all right, Kels. I promise,' he whispered. She'd be safe in his arms. Always.

And eventually she stopped shaking. Curled her arms round him. 'Thanks, Matt. For being here. For…well. You know.'

'Any time.' He dropped a kiss on her hair. It was meant to be a friendly, comforting kiss. Except her hair felt like silk against his lips. She smelled of coconut. Mouthwatering. He wanted to taste her, feel her skin against his mouth.

'I'm sorry I woke you,' she said.

'Not a problem.' Though that wasn't the absolute truth. There *was* a problem. A growing one. They were naked in bed together again. Skin to skin. Soft and warm. And that

massage he'd given her a few days ago had made him even
more aware of the effect she had on him. How much she
turned him on. How much he wanted her.

His right hand was resting on the curve of her hip. How
easy it would be to let his hand wander. Drift along the
curve. Stroke her skin. And how easy it would be to let his
left hand tip her face up towards him. Near enough to
lower his mouth to hers.

Uh. He'd promised himself he wouldn't push her. That
he'd give her time to get over the PTSD and be back to her
normal self before he declared himself. Making love with
her now would be taking advantage of her when she was
at her most vulnerable. It was wrong, wrong, *wrong*.

But his promise was getting more difficult to keep by
the second. He was just too aware of her clean scent, the
softness of her skin—and how much he wanted to touch
her. How much he wanted her to touch him. How much he
wanted to let the friction between their bodies chase her
nightmares away.

He'd better go now. Before he did something they'd
both regret. 'Better?' he asked softly.

'A bit.'

A bit was good. Well, not good exactly, but better than
the screaming nightmares. Now he'd remove himself from
temptation. Leave her in peace.

But then she did something that shattered all his good
intentions. She turned her face into his chest and kissed it.

Just when he'd convinced himself that it had been his
imagination trying to con him that it was reality, and he was
about to say goodnight and leave her to go back to sleep,
she did it again.

Kissed him.

Just the lightest brush of her lips against his skin. And

it turned every muscle in his legs to sand. No way was he able to get out of her bed. Not now. That light, light kiss had snapped the bonds of his self-control. He couldn't hold himself back any more: he did what he'd been aching to do. Stroked the curve of her buttocks.

Lord, her skin was so soft. So warm. A perfect curve. And his sigh of pleasure was out before he could stop it.

'Matt.'

'Yes?' Oh, bad. His voice was about an octave deeper than usual. And if she let her right hand drift down his body, she'd know for sure just what state he was in. Aroused. Fully aroused. *Achingly* aroused. Give it another minute and he wouldn't even be able to string a sentence together.

Her right hand moved. Stroked down his hipbone, just as he'd done to her. And he was definitely having the auditory version of hallucinations—there was a word for it, he was sure, but for the life of him he couldn't think of it right now. Her voice couldn't possibly sound husky and sensual. She couldn't be as turned on as he was.

There was one way to find out. Let his left hand wander down a bit. Cup her breasts.

Uh. He definitely shouldn't have thought of that. All the blood in his brain retaliated by rushing southwards.

Oh, Lord. Now her hand was drifting across his abdomen.

Busted. Big time. There was no way in hell she could fail to notice how hard he was.

'You drove me crazy with that massage,' she whispered.

That made two of them. He'd been tingling all over himself. Wanting to make it more intimate. Wanting to slide his hands between her thighs. Wanting to touch her and make her float in pleasure.

'I've been thinking about it. A lot,' she said.

Yep. He was with her all the way there. But the only sound his mouth would give up was a slurred, 'Uh.'

'Have you tried it out on your patients?'

'Nuh.' Oh, man. This was bad. Speaking troglodyte: it was hardly the way to impress the girl of your dreams. Especially one as bright as Kelsey.

'So it's just me?'

'Uh.' Bad, bad, bad. He'd gone way beyond coherent speech.

Another of those soft little kisses on his chest. Could she feel how fast and hard his heart was beating? Did she have any idea what she was doing to him?

Then she moved, and Matt nearly went into heart failure. If she hadn't known before, she definitely knew now. Because she was kneeling astride him. And there was no mistaking his body's reaction to hers. Not when her sex was actually resting against his, and he could feel just how hot she was. Just one small movement would sheathe him deep inside her. Where he wanted to be more than anything else in the world.

Her hands were on the pillow either side of his head. What he would have given for a soft glow of light, so he could see her. His imagination was supplying a pretty good picture but, oh, he wanted to see her. Touch her. Taste her.

She bent lower, so her breasts brushed against his chest.

In Matt's experience, women's nipples were only that hard if they were cold or if they were aroused. In Kelsey's bed it definitely wasn't cold. And when she rocked her hips and her body glided across his, he could feel how damp she was, too.

Which meant he wasn't alone in the way he was feeling. She was just as turned on as he was. Wanted this. Needed this. Oh, please. Now, now, now.

And then her mouth brushed lightly over his.

It was all he could do to stop himself grabbing her, flipping her onto her back and pushing deep inside her. His self-control was hanging by a thread thinner than spider silk. A whisper could blow it away.

'Ke…' Nope. The words weren't going to come out. No way could his vocal cords utter the words he knew he should say. *Are you sure about this? You're upset. Emotional. I can't take advantage of you like this. You'll regret it in the morning. You'll hate me for it. I'll hate myself for it, too.*

But his inner Tarzan was beating his chest and yelling incredibly loudly, *She's mine! All mine! Yes!*

And he knew he didn't stand a chance in hell of being a gentleman.

Matt was going to tell her to stop. Kelsey knew that. But she couldn't stop, not now. She'd been on a slow burn since he'd given her that back massage. Although her mind was perfectly aware that later was going to be excruciatingly awkward, her body just wasn't listening to anything her brain had to say. Not when Matt was lying beneath her, his erection pressing against her. She wanted him too much.

There was only one way to stop him being sensible. She kissed him again, this time nipping gently at his lower lip until he opened his mouth and let her deepen the kiss. A tremor rippled through his body, and she mentally punched a fist in the air. Yes. He wanted this as much as she did.

Then his hands came up to cup her breasts. His thumbs rubbed against her nipples, teasing the hard peaks.

This was it. No return. The last chance to say no.

Except she didn't want to say no. She didn't want *him* to say no either.

She wanted Matt. Inside her. Now.

She rocked her pelvis over him and was rewarded with

another shiver. And then she lifted herself slightly, slid her hand between them, and guided him to where ahe wanted him.

'Ke—' he began, but the word broke off as she lowered herself onto him. Slid down on him until he was sheathed inside her, right to the hilt. And Lord, Lord, Lord, it felt good.

He exhaled sharply, and his fingers tightened against her breasts.

Oh, yes. He was big and strong and hard—and he was *all hers*.

'Later,' she whispered. They'd talk later. But now she just wanted to feel. To lose herself in the way his body moved against hers.

He must have guessed what she was thinking because he shifted so that he was almost sitting, wrapped his arms round her and kissed her. Hard. She opened her mouth, letting him explore hers.

Immediately he gentled the kiss, and it almost broke her heart. It was as if he was telling her he knew how fragile she was right now. A promise that he wasn't going to hurt her. A promise that this would be good for both of them.

She was glad that he'd moved. So she could feel the strength of his body, his broad shoulders and the muscles that tapered down towards his narrow waist. He worked out, sure, but most of his muscles came from the physical side of his job. Like hers. Going to the gym was a wind-down for both of them. She loved swimming with him, spotting him on the weights, running on the treadmill with him. Just as she loved tramping through the Derbyshire dales with him. Or even slobbing on the sofa with him, resting her feet in his lap while they watched a film or sharing a tub of ice cream.

But she'd had no idea that it could be like this between

them. Making love with Matt was like nothing she'd ever known. It hadn't been this intense for her before, even with Danny. This burning need to have him deeper, deeper. To touch him. Taste him. Feel the texture of his skin beneath her mouth and tongue and teeth.

Her hands fisted briefly in his hair—the shaggy, slightly over-long style that on anyone else would look scruffy but on Matt just looked plain sexy. Especially first thing in the morning, when he hadn't shaved. Right now, she would have loved to switch the bedside light on, see if his face was blurred by desire. See herself reflected in his blue, blue eyes. See his beautiful mouth tracking over her shoulder and down one breast. Watch him suckling her.

But turning the light on might shock him into realising what they were doing. Shock him back into being her sensible flatmate and best friend. And she didn't want that. She wanted him as her lover. Here, now.

And tomorrow.

She jammed the thought back. No. She'd done that before. Made plans for a future. A future that had been wrecked by three little letters. A mess like the ones she had to clear up every single week. Never again.

But tonight—oh, they'd have tonight. She'd tell him with her body what she knew she could never tell him in words. That she wanted him. Needed him. Desired him.

Loved him.

Again, she pushed the thought away. No. She couldn't be in love with Matt. She'd made a very solemn promise to herself—that she'd never fall in love again. That she'd never be at risk of losing someone. That she'd never have to pick up the splintered pieces of her life again.

'Kelsey,' he murmured in her ear. 'Beautiful.'

She shivered as his mouth tracked down the sensitive

cord at the side of her neck and back up again, so his breath fanned her ear. 'Take my breath away. So lovely.' He groaned. 'Can't do whole sentences. Scrambled brain.'

Yeah. She knew that feeling. 'Me, too.' She rocked over him, gripping his shoulders as he kissed along the line of her collarbone. 'Driving me crazy.' Relentless pressure. Rising, rising, rising. She needed more. More.

Oh, more.

She realised she'd spoken aloud when he said, 'Me, too,' his voice guttural with desire.

And then she stopped thinking altogether as he took her over the edge.

'Matt. Yes!' she yelled, and his mouth jammed over hers again, cutting off the needy whimpers.

Breathing each other's breath. Feeling each other's heart pounding. Feeling the ripples of pleasure spreading through her body, echoed in his.

This was good. More than good. And she didn't want it to stop.

Ever.

CHAPTER TEN

MATT woke with Kelsey sprawled all over him, and a smile a mile wide. This was the perfect start to the day, waking up next to the woman he loved. He lay there for a moment, just enjoying the feel of her skin against his and the way she was cuddled into him.

This felt so right. Like coming home. For all he knew, it could be raining outside, but the sun was definitely shining on him. Because last night had been everything he'd dreamed about—and more. He knew now that what he felt for Kelsey was more than he'd ever feel about anyone for the rest of his life.

The first time between them shouldn't have been that good. It should have been exploring. Tentative. Maybe even a bit awkward.

But they'd been so in tune. As if they'd known instinctively what each other liked—the right pressure, the right speed, the right everything.

Absolutely perfect.

'I love you, Kelsey,' he whispered. 'And I just hope you're ready to hear it.'

He shifted slightly so he could see her bedside clock. Ah, hell. He had to leave the house in twenty minutes.

So should he leave her to sleep, or wake her? On a normal day, it wouldn't even be a question—her day shift started two hours after his and she wasn't always up before he left.

But today wasn't a normal morning.

It was the morning after they'd made love.

If he left her to sleep, she might think that last night didn't mean anything to him. He could leave her a note, but he wanted to tell her face to face just how much it had meant. It was too important to leave scribbled down on a piece of paper she might not see straight away. But if he woke her... Apart from the fact she'd had a broken night from her nightmare and they hadn't exactly had a great deal of sleep afterwards, they really didn't have enough time to talk about this properly before he had to go to work.

Caught between a rock and a hard place.

So he'd try for the middle ground. Tell her how he felt and promise to talk about it properly tonight when they were back from their shifts.

Wriggling out from her arms without waking her was one of the hardest things he'd done. Especially as his body didn't want to leave the soft warm body draped over it. There was a quick and dirty fight between his libido and his common sense—his common sense—won. Just.

He padded downstairs, switched on the kettle, then returned upstairs for a swift, quiet shower and shave and pulled on his work clothes. He made them both a mug of tea, then carried the mugs up to Kelsey's room.

He rapped on the door. 'Kels? You awake?'

'Uh?'

'Hey, sleepyhead.' He opened the door with his elbow, walked in, put the mugs on her bedside table, and sat on the edge of her bed. 'I brought you some tea. I have to leave for my shift in about ten minutes, and I didn't want to go without saying goodbye.'

She rubbed a hand across her face. 'Um. Thanks.' She pulled the duvet round her to cover her breasts, and sat up.

She was shy? After what they'd done last night? Oh, bless. Matt smiled and took her hand. 'Hey. You all right?'

'Mmm.' She wriggled against her pillows, clearly feeling awkward. 'Matt. Last night…it shouldn't have happened.'

Uh-oh. He'd been prepared for a bit of awkwardness between them this morning, but not this. He'd been so sure she'd felt the same way as he did. Had he read it wrong?

'Last night was a long time in the making,' he said quietly. It had only been when his body had been sheathed in hers that he'd realised just how long he'd wanted to do that. He didn't let her hand go, and he kept his gaze firmly on hers. 'Though I admit, I feel bad about taking advantage of you. You had a nightmare and I wanted to comfort you—except I leapt on you instead.'

She flushed. 'Actually, I was the one who did the leaping.'

Mmm, and he remembered just how, too. The way she'd touched him. The way she'd straddled him. He grinned. 'Hey. I don't have a problem with you taking charge. I'm a modern guy. My ego can stand it.'

She shook her head. 'Matt. We can't do this.'

'Too late. We already did.' He lifted her hand to his mouth and kissed each fingertip in turn, holding her gaze. He was about to tell her that he loved her—but then he saw the panic in her face and bit the words back. Now wasn't the time. If he told her right now, she'd run. They needed time to talk this through. And he had an ambulance crew waiting for him; he couldn't just forget his responsibilities and concentrate on her. Even though, right now, he wanted to.

But there was one subject that couldn't wait. 'There's one thing we do have to talk about before I go to work.' He cleared his throat. 'We didn't use a condom last night.' They'd both been too carried away to think about birth control. He'd only thought about it in the shower.

Colour rushed into her face. 'Um, no. Look, I don't sleep around. Neither do you.' She shrugged and pulled her hand free. 'So it's not a problem.'

Oh, but it might be. 'Actually, I wasn't thinking about STDs.' He waited for the penny to drop, but she was clearly in denial. 'I was thinking about babies.'

She shook her head. 'That's not a problem either. I was having hassles with my periods and my GP put me on the Pill months ago.'

Oh. He hadn't known that.

She wrapped the duvet even more firmly round herself. 'You'd better go, or you'll be late for your shift.'

For a brief moment he didn't care about his shift. Didn't care about the job that had been the centre of his world for—well, for too long. What he really wanted to do was kiss her goodbye. Like a lover. Full of promise. But she'd put a brick wall up between them—faster than he'd ever thought she could. A brick wall he had to knock down before she added a second one in front of it plus barbed wire, then built a nuclear bunker behind it.

He had people depending on him. People he couldn't let down. He really ought to get going. But he couldn't leave her like this. He just couldn't.

'Kels, we can't leave it like this.'

'Like what?'

'You know like what.' He sighed. 'Look, last night happened. We'll have to deal with it. You can't put your head in the sand about it like you're doing about your PTSD.'

'I don't have my head in the sand about anything.' She glared at him.

'Yes, you do. You've been having nightmares. And it's going on way longer than it should do.' He knew he ought to be treading carefully, but he couldn't stop his frustration boiling over. 'When are you going to admit that you're not superwoman—that you're human?'

'That's rich, coming from you!' she snapped.

'OK. So we both have a save-the-world complex. That's why I'm a paramedic and you're a firefighter.' He brushed her protest aside. 'But you need to start admitting that you have a problem. It's not a weakness, Kels. It's something you need to sort out or it's going to get worse—and you're the one who's going to suffer most.' He folded his arms. 'Did you have nightmares like this after the accident with Danny?'

She flinched as if he'd hit her. 'The accident's got nothing to do with it.'

'Hasn't it? Last night, you told me you'd failed. And I don't think you just meant about the kids. It's how you feel about Danny, isn't it?'

'Don't be ridiculous.'

'After the accident,' Matt continued, ignoring the anger on her face, 'you wanted to nurse him back to health. He wouldn't let you. He made you give him his ring back. And you've never stopped feeling guilty about that—never stopped feeling that you failed him. Even though you didn't just walk away or take the easy option—you did your best to change his mind—you felt you didn't do enough.'

'It's none of your business.'

'Yes, it is. Because you're tearing yourself apart, Kels, and I can't just stand by and see you hurting. I want to help.'

She scowled. 'More like, you want to take over.'

'No, I want to help,' he corrected. 'You need to face what's happening instead of running away from it.'

Her hands fisted in the duvet. 'I'm not running away from anything!'

'No? Then tell me why you've never got involved with anyone since Danny.'

'That's rubbish. Of course I've got involved.'

He shook his head. 'You've hardly dated. You're the first one to accept a party invitation but you always make sure you don't get too close to anyone.' He paused. 'Even me. Because what happened last night…it's been between us for a long time. We both knew it and we've both been avoiding it. Running scared. But I'm not running any more, Kelsey. And it's time you stopped, too. It's time you faced the past and dealt with it.'

'You're being completely ridiculous.'

'I wish I was,' Matt said, and the fight suddenly left him. His shoulders sagged. 'Until you've dealt with whatever guilt you feel about Danny, you're not going to be able to move on.'

'What about you and Cassie?'

He shrugged. 'It's not an issue. She wanted me to be someone else—someone I couldn't be. I don't have a nice steady nine-to-five job. My hours aren't always social and I can't just leave a patient in the middle of treatment. She couldn't accept that, and I didn't want to be trapped in some stuffy office job. We weren't right for each other— I can see that now and I wish her well.' His eyes met hers. 'I know you're still in touch with Danny. Maybe you should talk to him. *Really* talk. Clear up all the things you didn't resolve years ago.'

'I don't have any unresolved issues,' she said tightly.

This was going from bad to worse. She wasn't going to

budge on this. And he was needed somewhere else. He stood up, shaking his head. 'Have it your way. I'm going to be late for my shift.'

And even though it killed him to do it, he walked away.

Kelsey pulled the duvet over her head as she heard the front door close behind Matt. What the hell had she done?

Last night she'd been in despair. Haunted by the nightmare that seemed to be creeping into every moment of her life. And even though she'd tried to muffle her sobs, Matt had heard. Come to comfort her. Held her close.

And, Lord, it had felt good to be in his arms. Warm and safe—nothing could hurt her when Matt was with her.

She'd snuggled against him. Kissed him. No, face facts, she'd thrown herself at him. And he was a man. Of course he wasn't going to say no when she'd straddled him and made it very clear that she was his for the taking. Sex on a plate.

Worse, she'd even told him how crazy he'd driven her with that massage.

He'd said the 'me, too' bit, but—well, that had just been sex talking, hadn't it?

This was the worst thing she'd ever, ever done. Matt was her best friend. And she'd just wrecked the best friendship she'd ever had. They'd had their first real fight. And everything was different now they'd made love. They couldn't go back to their old easiness, the teasing and the fun and the laughter—not now they'd had sex. They couldn't curl up on the sofa together with a tub of ice cream and a good film. No more of Matt's wonderful foot massages. Getting hot and sweaty together at the gym would be too much of a reminder of the way they'd got hot and sweaty in a much more private situation.

She flipped over onto her stomach and yelled her frustration into her pillow. How stupid, stupid, *stupid* she'd been. Everything she'd had with Matt—the perfect life— she'd thrown away. For one night of sex.

One night of exquisite sex, admittedly, but still just sex.

If it hadn't happened, everything would be fine now. They wouldn't be fighting. She wouldn't be feeling guilty.

Guilty. Was that what was really behind her nightmares? she wondered as she washed her hair and showered. Was it true that feeling she'd failed Mikey and Lucy had reminded her of how she'd failed Danny, too?

Ah, hell. Maybe Matt was right. Maybe she did need to talk to Danny. And maybe she needed to talk to someone about the nightmares. Stop thinking she could do it all on her own. Admit that there was a problem and she needed help.

She glanced at the clock. Another hour until her shift. Well, she didn't want to wait that long. If she was going to do it, she wanted to do it now. Before she lost her nerve.

She picked up her mobile phone and flicked through her list of numbers. When she came to Ray's, she speed-dialled it. Please, let him be up. She knew he wouldn't be on the school run because it was still August and the kids weren't back yet. Please, let him be up and not out with the dog or what have you...

'Hello?'

She sagged back in her seat in relief. 'Guv, it's Kelsey. I was wondering. Can we have a word?'

'Sure. After roll-call?'

The start of every shift, where they found out which vehicle they were riding in and which position. No. She couldn't handle it then. She couldn't face the crew first. 'How about I shout you a coffee at the café down the road, in about a quarter of an hour's time?'

'OK.' She could hear the concern in his voice. 'Are you all right, Brains?'

'Yes. Well, not really,' she admitted. 'That's what I want to talk to you about.'

'I'll be there waiting for you,' he said. 'With coffee. And a bacon butty.'

Tears pricked her eyelids. He cared. Ray really cared about his crew. She should be pleased. Relieved. Why the hell did she feel like crying? 'Thanks, guv.' Her voice sounded rusty to her. As if she were slowly grinding to a halt. Seizing up. 'See you there.'

She drove to the station on autopilot. Parked. Walked down to the café. And Ray was there, as promised, with a cup of strong coffee and a bacon sandwich on the place opposite him.

'You look like hell,' he said as she slid into the seat.

'I feel it,' she admitted. 'Guv…what you said yesterday.'

'You're having problems coming to terms with the Bannington fire?' he guessed.

She nodded. And just admitting it suddenly made it easier to talk. To say the words that had been stuck in her head for so long. 'I get nightmares. They creep up on me, even during the day. I just see that moment when the fire came through the panelling and cut me off from those kids. I hear it. I hear *them*. I see their faces. I see…' She stopped, the words choked off by the horror in her head. She couldn't speak about that sickening moment when they'd realised she couldn't save them. That they were going to die in the fire.

'Does Matt know?' Ray asked gently.

She swallowed. 'Yeah.'

Ray's face tightened. 'So why the hell hasn't he done anything about it?'

Oh, no. She wasn't having Matt blamed for something that was all her own fault. Though at the same time it warmed her heart. Despite her accusations, Matt *hadn't* gone behind her back and spoken to her boss about it. 'He's tried. Believe me, he's tried. I just wasn't ready to admit I had a problem.'

'In Egypt, huh?'

The hoary old joke. In de Nile. Denial. 'Yes.'

'So what changed?'

Matt. Making love.

Her face heated. No way was she talking about *that*. Way too personal. 'It just did. And I'm sorry, you're right. I put the crew at risk. I shouldn't have done it. And, um, I'll give you my formal resignation later today.'

'Absolutely not.'

She narrowed her eyes. Had she heard that right? 'You're not accepting my resignation? Why, when I've let you down?'

'You haven't let me down. I've got money on you being one of the first female station officers in our area,' Ray said. 'And I only bet on sure things.'

She couldn't take it in. 'But I've just proved I can't handle it.'

'No. You've been strong enough to admit that you're having a problem. A problem that can be dealt with. We can get you help, Kelsey,' Ray said, reaching over to squeeze her hand briefly. 'Like I told you, you're not the first and you won't be the last.'

She gulped the threatening tears back. 'I don't know what to say.'

'You're on sick leave, as of now,' he said. 'I can explain to the watch if you want. Or you can do it yourself when you come back. But we're all going to be rooting for you and we're definitely expecting you back.' He smiled. 'I mean, how's the watch going to hold our own in quiz nights without the brainiest firefighter on our team?'

Then the tears came—an unexpected rush that had her choking. Without comment, Ray handed her a handkerchief. Waited until she'd calmed down again. And then squeezed her hand once more.

'Want me to call Matt?' he asked.

'No. He's probably on a shout by now.' And she really couldn't face him. Not until she had her head straight.

'Go and see your GP,' Ray said.

She nodded. 'Guv—don't put me on sick leave. Please. I'll go crazy if I sit at home with nothing to do but brood about it. I'll get an appointment with my GP for tomorrow during the day, so it doesn't interfere with my shift.'

'Hey. Your health is important,' Ray protested.

'I know. And I'm going to do something about it.' She swallowed hard.

'OK. You'll be fine, I know,' he said softly. 'And you've got Matt. He'll help.'

'We had a fight.' She clapped her hand over her mouth, horrified at what she'd just blurted out.

Ray shrugged. 'You'll make it up. He'd walk barefoot over burning coals for you, you know.'

She flushed. 'We're just friends.'

He said nothing. He didn't need to: his expression said it all for him. That Matt would do anything for her. Move mountains, fight dragons. Anything.

Maybe it was time she fought, too. Conquered her past. Only she'd do it as part of a team instead of on her own. Side by side with Matt.

But first she had to talk to Danny.

CHAPTER ELEVEN

'YOU'RE twitching,' Dale said.

'Am not.'

'Had a fight with Kelsey?'

Matt scowled. 'You say a word to anyone back at Base, and you're catfood.'

Dale grinned. 'I don't need to. You were late for your shift, even though you drove instead of cycled, and you slammed your locker door this morning. Twice. Everyone's guessed something's up.'

Matt took a swig of coffee. No way was he going to admit exactly what had happened. That was between him and Kelsey. 'I screwed up,' he muttered.

'Then say the s-word. Buy the girl some flowers or some chocolates. She'll forgive you.'

Would she? 'I'm not so sure,' Matt admitted. 'I said some pretty harsh things.' True things—but they'd been harsh. Things that he knew she'd have found it hard to listen to. And his timing had been way off. He'd let his frustrations rip when she had been at her most vulnerable. Which made him the most selfish bastard on the planet.

'She's probably feeling as bad as you do. Why don't you

ring her and make it up?' Dale winked at him. 'And I promise not to listen in.'

'Hmm.' Matt wasn't convinced she'd even talk to him.

'Just do it, will you? For me, if not for yourself,' Dale pleaded. 'I can't stand having you in a mood like this for the entire shift.' He pulled onto a side road and parked. 'I'll yell if we get a shout.'

Matt climbed out of the ambulance. He leaned against the side of the van, took his mobile phone from his pocket and called Kelsey's number. She might be on a shout herself. Well, if she was and she didn't answer her phone, he'd text her. Say he was sorry. And hope to hell that everything could be smoothed over.

She answered within three rings. 'Hello?'

She sounded wary. Not surprising. She would've seen his number on the screen of her mobile phone and probably thought he was going to have another go at her. But at least she was talking to him.

'Hey. Just calling.' To say he was sorry. To tell her he loved her. *No.* Now wasn't the right time. 'To see if you're OK,' he said carefully.

'Yeah.'

Was that 'yeah, I know why you're calling' or 'yeah, I'm OK'? He took a deep breath. Time to bite the bullet. Say the right words. 'I'm sorry. I shouldn't have gone off at the deep end this morning.'

'It's OK. You had a point.' She paused. 'I'm sorry, too. I've been stupid.'

'Stubborn, yes; stupid, no,' he corrected.

'I talked to Ray. And I've got an appointment with my doctor tomorrow.'

'Good.' His heart lifted. Maybe everything was going to be all right. 'I'll go with you. For moral support,' he offered.

'I'll be fine.'

Which was a no. She didn't want him there. And she sounded cool. So were they making up—or was she cementing a few more courses of bricks on top of the wall between them? There was only one way to find out. 'Did you call Danny?'

'Not yet.'

She sounded even frostier. Hell. Why had he opened his big mouth? 'I guess I'll see you tonight, then.'

'Yeah.'

If only he could see her face, work out what she was thinking from her expression. 'We need to talk, Kels,' he said softly.

'Yeah.'

That definitely sounded more like 'no'. 'I'll cook dinner. Peace offering.'

There was a long pause—so long that he felt panic rising in his gut. Then she spoke. 'OK. I'll buy ice cream. Peace offering.'

Ice cream? Ha. What he *really* wanted for dessert was her. But he'd already messed things up by rushing her. Now he'd wait until she was ready. Until she'd resolved everything with Danny. 'Kels...' But then he heard the Tannoy warbling in the background.

'Got a shout. Better go.' And the phone went dead.

Just as he pressed the button to end the call, Dale leaned out of the window. 'Got a shout.'

Probably the same one as Kelsey. Well, they were professionals. Whatever the problems between them, they could still work together as a team.

He hoped.

'What's the shout?' Matt asked, climbing into the passenger seat.

'Elderly woman trapped under bus. The fire crew are on their way to extract her.' Dale gave him a sidelong look as he pulled back onto the road, the siren and lights going. 'So did you talk to her?'

'Yeah.'

'And?'

Matt shrugged.

Dale groaned. 'Tell me you said the s-word. As if you meant it.'

'Ye-es. And I'm cooking dinner tonight. Peace offering.'

'Better do flowers as well,' Dale advised. 'Or chocolate. There was this survey in the paper the other day. Did you know women prefer chocolate to sex?'

'I didn't say I was having sex with Kelsey.' Though Matt could feel his face heating. That was what they'd done, wasn't it?

Well, what *she'd* done. He'd been making love. He'd hoped she had been doing the same. Until this morning, when she'd blocked him out.

'Lighten up,' Dale said.

'Yeah. We have a job to do.'

They drove into the city centre. The police were directing traffic around the scene of the accident, and the fire crew were already there, putting the lifting gear in place to get the bus off the elderly woman.

Automatically, Matt looked for Kelsey. Even with her back to him, he recognised her. And he was shocked by how much he yearned to touch her. Not here, not now, he reminded himself, and headed for the bus.

A quick glance showed him that the old lady's legs were trapped under one of the back wheels of the bus. OK. Now was the bit where he had to talk to Kelsey— with her firefighter hat on. Keep it professional, he told himself sharply. No personal stuff. 'Hi. What happened?' he asked her.

'Slipped under the bus while she was getting on. The driver didn't see it happen and moved off,' Kelsey said economically.

'How long has she been there?'

'About fifteen minutes.'

Which meant that her circulation could be compromised—they needed to get her out fast to avoid any more damage to her tissues. He nodded acknowledgement, then knelt down by his patient. 'Hello, love. My name's Matt. I'm a paramedic. I'm going to check you over and get you to hospital,' he said to the old lady. 'What's your name?'

'Betty.' She was clearly in pain but smiled at him. A real trouper, just like his great-aunt, he thought.

'OK, Betty, we'll get you out of there. Are you taking any medication?'

'No, I'm healthy as a horse. At least, I was,' she said.

'As soon as the fire brigade have lifted the bus, we're going to get you onto a rescue board and get you to the ambulance,' he told her. 'Hey, Kelsey. How long d'you reckon it'll take?'

'Another ten minutes or so. I'm going as fast as I can.'

Ah, hell. He wasn't criticising her. She was good at her job. 'I know you are. Thanks.'

Their eyes met for a moment. And the depth of pain in her eyes made him want to hold her. Soothe her. Tell her everything was going to be all right.

Except he couldn't. He already had a patient to sort out. And he needed Kelsey to help him.

He turned back to the elderly woman. 'I'm going to put a collar on you, Betty, to keep your neck nice and still.'

'In case of cervical spine damage.' He must have looked

surprised, because she explained, 'Used to be a nurse myself. In the war. This is nothing compared to what some of our lads went through.'

'You're a brave woman.' He squeezed her hand. 'Did you bang your head at all?'

'Don't think so.'

Good. That was one less thing to worry about.

'We had girl firefighters in the war, too,' Betty said. 'With buckets of sand on the tops of buildings, to put the fires from the incendiary bombs out before they took hold.'

'Sand's good. It means the fire can't get to the oxygen,' Kelsey said. 'Though we tend to use protein foam now. It smells utterly disgusting.'

'Tell me about it,' Matt said. 'When she's been using that stuff, it's definitely her turn to do the laundry.'

'You're married?' Betty asked.

He exchanged a glance with Kelsey. And he couldn't read her face at all. Was that an 'over my dead body' look, or was there a hint of wistfulness in her expression? Did she want to be with him as much as he wanted to be with her?

Ah, hell. This wasn't the time or the place.

'We're housemates,' Kelsey explained with a smile.

Yeah. And it wasn't enough for him.

As soon as the bus was lifted, he looked round for Dale.

'The bus driver's in shock. Dale's dealing with him,' Kelsey said. 'Want me to help?'

Well, she knew what she was doing. She'd been on courses. And he knew she was sensible enough to follow his instructions. 'Thanks. On my count, we'll lift her onto the board. One, two, three, lift.'

They worked together so well as a team, Matt thought as they slid Betty onto the rescue board. They were in tune.

Had been, right from the start. Please, God, let their personal life work out as well as their professional one.

He switched into work mode and assessed Betty as they lifted her.

'Can you try and move your legs for me?' he asked. 'Wiggle your toes.'

To his relief, she was able to wiggle her toes, and her legs felt warm.

'My left leg feels very heavy,' Betty said.

Unsurprisingly, Matt thought as he assessed her leg. 'Your patella's taken a bit of a hard knock.' It was virtually mush, and the skin and muscle were torn. Though it seemed to be the only real damage—her breathing and heart rate were fine. He could hear air entry on both sides of her chest, so a tension pneumothorax was unlikely, too. 'Does it hurt anywhere else? Any pain in your chest, your back?'

'No, just my leg,' Betty said. 'It feels a bit heavy.'

It hurt like hell, in other words—but her generation believed in a stiff upper lip. 'I can give you some pain relief,' Matt said, 'as your obs are fine.'

'Thank you,' she said.

He quickly gave her some pain relief, then he and Kelsey lifted her to the ambulance. Dale was already there, seeing to the bus driver.

'We'll get you to hospital. They'll take some X-rays to see what's going on, and the orthopods will sort your leg out. Dale's going to stay in the back with you while I drive,' he said. 'Kels, thanks for your help.'

'No problem.' To his surprise, she actually reached over and squeezed his arm. Very briefly, but it was contact. Personal contact. 'See you later.'

'Yeah.' He smiled back at her. Maybe, just maybe, this was going to work out.

When they'd handed Betty over to the emergency department team, the rest of the day turned out to be crazy. A bad back, where a man had bent down to get something from the floor and couldn't move his head or his legs. 'Could be a muscle spasm or it could be a trapped nerve,' Matt said. 'With injuries like this, your back muscles tense up to support it. It might be that if you have a muscle relaxant, you'll be fine, but we'll take you in. Roll over, nice and straight; keep your legs as straight as you can.'

'My side hurts.'

'I know. But we'll get you into the emergency department and they'll be able to take a better look at you.' He and Dale manoeuvred the man onto the stretcher and strapped him in. 'Not that we think you'll run away,' he said with a grin. 'But we want to keep you as still as we can so we don't do any more damage to your back.'

'I'll never live it down at the rugby club. Stretchered off for picking up a mug of tea from the floor,' the man said ruefully.

'We promise not to tell if you don't,' Dale teased.

Matt meant to give Kelsey a ring during his lunch-break, but they had back-to-back shouts. An elderly lady who'd fallen and bumped her head had seemed very confused, and needed to be taken to hospital for a CT scan to check she hadn't done any serious damage. A toddler with an allergic reaction, two more RTAs—neither of which were serious enough to call the fire brigade but both had potential whiplash cases that needed to go into hospital for assessment—and finally a woman who'd been having contractions all day but hadn't wanted to go in to hospital until her husband came home.

'I'm out of here,' Matt said when he and Dale finally got back to the ambulance station.

'Don't forget the flowers,' Dale teased.

He didn't. First stop was the florist's, where he ordered a hand-tied bouquet of bright pink roses, freesias and lilies, then a super-fast dash round the supermarket for prawns, lemon grass and stirfry vegetables, along with a punnet of raspberries in case she forgot to buy the ice cream she'd promised, back to the florist's to pick up the bouquet and, finally, home.

Please, just let her talk to him. Let them sort this out, he prayed.

Kelsey was already in the kitchen, with a half-drunk mug of tea in front of her and one of her ubiquitous puzzle magazines. 'Want a coffee?' she asked, looking up.

'No, you're all right. I've probably drunk too many cups today anyway.'

She raised an eyebrow. 'Flowers?'

'For you. Yeah. It's traditional when you apologise to a woman. You give her flowers.' Awkwardly, he handed the bouquet to her.

'You didn't have to. But thank you.' She buried her face in the flowers. 'Mmm. They smell gorgeous.'

While she arranged them in a vase, Matt poured them both a glass of wine and cooked the stirfry. She was concentrating on the flowers rather than talking to him, but he decided to leave it for the time being. At least she was still in the same room as him. And maybe she'd open up to him over dinner.

'So how was your day?' he asked as he dished up.

'OK. Yours?'

'OK.' They were being so polite. And he hated this pussyfooting around. Time to bite the bullet. 'How did Ray react this morning?'

She took a deep breath. 'He suggested taking sick leave. But I couldn't handle that—I'd rather be busy.'

'Yeah.' He could understand that. He'd be the same. Though he noticed that she was toying with her food. 'Kels, you're supposed to be eating.'

'I'm too jittery tonight,' she admitted. 'This whole thing…I've been doing a lot of thinking today.'

Uh-oh. He wasn't sure if he liked the sound of this or not. 'Want to share?' he asked carefully.

She pushed her plate away. 'I was so mad at you this morning. What you said—'

'I'm sorry,' he cut in. 'I know I pushed you too hard, and I shouldn't have done. I shouldn't have said what I did.'

'What made it worse is that you're right. I still feel guilty about Danny. If we hadn't had that accident…well, you and me, we might never even have met.' She bit her lip. 'I'd have been a maths teacher, not a firefighter. I wouldn't be living in Sheffield. I'd have been married to Danny. And I might even have had a baby by now.'

He'd thought he'd known her so well. But he didn't have a clue right now what was going on in her head. Was she trying to tell him that she didn't want to be with him, that she wanted Danny? Was she saying that she regretted the choices she'd made, that she wanted to turn back the clock?

'The accident changed everything,' she said quietly. 'I gave Danny his ring back.'

'Because he asked you to.'

She shook her head. 'I should've tried harder. I failed him, Matt. I let him down. Just like I let everyone down at the Bannington fire.' She took a deep breath. 'I put my crewmates at risk. I went in there when I didn't have enough safety margin in my oxygen tank. But I knew the kids were in there. I knew they were scared. How could I have turned my back on them?'

'It's a decision you had to make. A tough one. Whatever you did, you would have lost,' Matt said gently. 'You did the best you could.'

'It wasn't enough. Like it wasn't enough, what I did for Danny.'

'Kels, you can't beat yourself up for that for the rest of your life. And you really have to talk to him. Get closure. Real closure.'

'Yeah. I know. I tried ringing him earlier but he was away on a course.' She shrugged. 'I've left a message at his hotel. Hopefully he'll call me tonight.'

And hopefully she'd come to a decision. Choose what she wanted.

Only, please let her choose *him*.

'What time's your doctor's appointment tomorrow?'

'Eleven.'

'Want me to come with you?' She'd turned him down when he'd offered earlier, but maybe now she'd accept his help.

She shook her head. 'Thanks, but I'll cope.'

He should have guessed she'd be self-contained, as always. She hated the idea of relying on anyone. 'At least you're admitting there's a problem now.'

'Yeah. And you're right, I've been getting flashbacks. They come out of nowhere. I see the flames.' She shuddered. 'I see their faces. Hear them scream. Hear the roar of the flames. It spins round and round and round, and it won't stop. When we get a shout to a school or college, I freeze. When we get a shout and kids are involved, it feels like hell. I can hardly get myself into the fire engine. God, even at the Chinese take-away—I heard the sizzling from the kitchen and it started a flashback. Even normal things aren't safe any more.' She shook her head. 'But I shouldn't be feeling like this, Matt. I'm a trained firefighter. I know what I'm doing.'

'Course you do.' He took her hand and squeezed it—then moved his hand away again. While he still could. Before he did something stupid like drag her into his arms and kiss her senseless. Now wasn't the time. 'I still think the PTSD goes back to your accident. The stuff I read said sometimes it takes years to come out. You were OK when Danny wasn't; and then at Bannington you were OK when…' When the kids weren't. 'It's known as survivor guilt.'

'I was so sure I was over the accident. I felt guilty for months afterwards, but I thought I'd worked it through. And now, after the fire…I dunno. I'm a mess. Emotional wreckage.' She took a swig of her wine. 'And you and me…I feel as if I've betrayed Danny.'

Was this her way of telling him he was her first lover since Danny?

That complicated things even more.

'You need to talk to him,' Matt said softly. 'Find out what *you* want.'

'That's the thing.' She took a shuddering breath. 'I think I know what I want—and then I think I'm wrong for wanting it.'

He took a deep breath. 'I'm your best friend.' He wanted to be more than that—a *lot* more than that—but if that was all she could offer him right now, he'd have to accept it. 'If you need me, I'm here for you. That's not going to change. Ever.'

'I hate myself for this. For being so…so weak.'

He smiled wryly. 'Weak is the last word I'd use to describe you, Kels. You'll be fine. You'll get through this. Just talk to Danny.' For *both* our sakes, he thought.

CHAPTER TWELVE

DANNY didn't ring her back on Wednesday evening. And since Kelsey had made it clear she didn't want Matt around for her doctor's appointment on Thursday morning, Matt headed for the gym instead. Took out his frustration on the weights. Ran for twenty minutes on the treadmill in an attempt to clear his head.

But it didn't work.

All he could think about was Kelsey. The way she'd felt in his arms. How soft her skin was. The silky texture of her hair. Her scent. The touch of her mouth on his body. The little murmurs of pleasure she'd made when he'd driven his body into hers.

Thank God she hadn't woken screaming last night. He'd gone to bed fully dressed, just in case. No way would he have left her to cry alone, but he also didn't trust himself to hold her skin to skin. Not now he knew what it was like to make love with her. His self-control wasn't *that* strong.

There were things she needed to sort out. Things he'd only complicate if he did what his body was urging him to do and made her his again. She needed to be sure what she wanted, and he just hoped to hell it was him.

He was messing about on the internet, trying to kill

time until Kelsey returned from the doctor's, when his mobile phone rang.

He glanced at the screen before he answered the call. *Kelsey.*

'Hi,' he said, trying to make his voice sound bright and cheerful.

'I've been trying to ring you for ages. But you're obviously on the net.'

Which meant their landline had been engaged. 'Yeah. Sorry.' He hadn't been expecting her to phone him. 'How did it go?'

'OK. My GP's sending me to see a specialist—I should get the appointment through tomorrow,' she said.

'That's good.' So why hadn't she come home? Was she avoiding him, or was he just being paranoid?

'Listen, um, I'm going shopping,' Kelsey told him. 'I'll probably go straight to my shift from Meadowhall.'

What? But Kelsey hated shopping. She especially hated huge malls like Meadowhall. It was definitely beginning to sound as if she was avoiding him.

Had she called Danny? Had they talked?

'Matt? You there?'

'Yeah.' He pulled his thoughts together with difficulty. 'Have fun. See you for breakfast maybe.'

'Yeah, maybe.'

This was going from bad to worse. She was supposed to have said 'yes', not 'maybe'.

'Hope you have a quiet shift.'

'You, too,' he said. And then the line went dead.

Matt banged his fists on the table and swore. This was going so wrong, it was untrue. He'd thought that today might be the start of a new beginning. Where Kelsey would take the first step towards sorting out her PTSD and talk to Danny, clear up her lingering guilt. And then finally she'd be free to take *their* relationship to a new level.

He knew he was on tenterhooks, but suddenly he began to wonder if he'd miscalculated. What if she didn't actually want him the way he wanted her?

Matt had no idea how he got through the rest of the afternoon. Or through the first call on his shift. He knew he was doing the right things medically—Dale would've picked him up on any mistakes—but he felt weirdly detached. He didn't have the usual connection with his patients. He was just doing a job. Going through the motions.

His heart was somewhere else.

Then his mobile phone rang.

He answered without bothering to look at the display. 'Matt Fraser.'

'Hey. It's me.'

Kelsey. His pulse speeded up, and he closed his eyes. He had to sound calm. Cool, collected. As if it was merely his best friend talking, not the woman he wanted most in the world. 'Hi. How are you doing?'

'I've just spoken to Danny.'

The moment he'd been waiting for. Dreading and wanting desperately at the same time. She'd talked to her ex-fiancé. Sorted things out. Please, please, let her have sorted things out.

He couldn't take in what she was saying, but one word seeped through his preoccupations.

Engaged.

What? She was going back to Danny? Their engagement was back on after all this time?

It was the last thing he'd expected. The woman he loved was getting married to someone else.

How the hell was he going to deal with this? Be nice. Be kind. Work his frustrations out on the machines at the gym again after his shift. But be nice for now, he told himself. She deserved happiness. And if Danny was what she wanted rather than him… Yeah, it hurt. But it'd hurt him more if she was miserable.

'I hope you'll both be very happy,' he said carefully.

'What? Matt, have you been taking a nip from the entonox?'

Entonox? He frowned. 'What are you talking about?'

'What are *you* talking about?'

Oh, man. Did she really want it spelt out? His heart had just shattered into tiny pieces. 'I was congratulating you on your engagement,' he said through gritted teeth.

She laughed.

She actually *laughed*.

'That just proves my point that men never listen. *I'm* not engaged, you dope. Danny is.'

'*What?*'

'Yeah. He'd been planning to ring me this week and tell me. But I got in first.'

Matt really couldn't take this in. So all those stupid, paranoid fears had been just that? Stupid, paranoid fears? Not fact at all? 'Danny's getting engaged. To someone else,' he said slowly.

'Yeah. We had a long talk. He's moved on with his life—he says he still loves me as a friend but he's not in love with me any more. He felt bad about finding someone else after he pushed me away, but he's not the same person now as he was when he asked *me* to marry him.'

Matt wanted to punch the air, whoop and do a dance. But that wouldn't be tactful if Kelsey was upset about it.

And he really couldn't tell from her voice whether she was relieved or distraught. 'Are you OK?' he asked carefully.

'I felt a bit…well…rejected, I suppose,' she admitted. 'When he first told me. But now…'

Matt only just stopped himself from yelling, *For God's sake, woman, tell me!*

'I suppose I feel a bit mixed up. In some ways I'm relieved. Danny's happy—and he deserves to find someone who'll make him happy.'

Someone who wasn't Kelsey. Yep. That worked for Matt, too.

'And I don't feel guilty any more about walking away. I mean, I didn't walk away of my own free will. I left because he wouldn't let me stay. But now I know it was the right thing for both of us. He says he feels that Jilly— that's his new fiancée—is his equal because she's only ever known him since he's been in a wheelchair, whereas with me he'd always have been thinking about how he used to be and feeling he wasn't good enough any more. Harking back to the past instead of moving forward. And now he's happy. His life's moved on.'

'And you—are you ready to move on, too?' The words were out before he could stop them. And Matt could have kicked himself. Now wasn't the time or the place to push.

'I think,' she said, 'we need to talk. Tomorrow morning. Over breakfast.'

He glanced at his watch. Breakfast. Which meant after the end of her shift, probably half-nine by the time she got home. Nearly fourteen hours away. How the hell was he going to last out for another fourteen hours? 'Kelsey?'

The Tannoy's warble cut in. 'Sorry, gotta go. There's a shout. I'll see you soon.'

And that was it. Matt was left staring at his phone, wondering what was going through her head and where they went from here.

He'd just got himself a coffee when the shout came.

'I reckon that coffee-machine's jinxed,' he said to Dale with a rueful grin. 'The second I touch it, we always seem to get a shout.' Though right now he could do with a really busy Thursday night. Something to keep his mind off Kelsey. 'What have we got, Dale?' Would it be the same shout as Kelsey's?

'Forty-year-old man, fell off a ladder in his back yard.'

Not the same shout as Kelsey's, then. They wouldn't need the fire brigade for this. 'That's a fair drop—at least ten feet. Do we know what he landed on?'

'Fence, then concrete.'

'Ouch.' It meant there was a likely risk of fractures, internal injuries and head injuries, depending on how the man had landed.

They switched on the sirens and lights and weaved through the traffic to the city outskirts.

Matt introduced himself quickly to the man groaning on the ground. 'What's your name, mate?'

'Patrick.'

'What happened?' Matt asked.

'Painting windows. Got the in-laws coming for a long weekend. Wanted to make the place look nice. Ladder slipped.'

Patrick wasn't talking in complete sentences, but that was probably because of the pain. He was certainly alert, which was good. Though he was also breathless, which wasn't such a good sign, Matt thought, assessing him.

'How did you land?'

'Fence. Fell onto driveway.'

Arrested fall. With the distance Patrick had travelled, almost certainly that meant fractures.

'Where does it hurt, Patrick?' Matt asked.

'Right side.'

'The side where you landed?'

He nodded, clearly hurting too much to talk.

'OK. I'm just going to check you over, then I'll give you something for the pain,' Matt said.

Patrick was getting more and more breathless; worse, there were no breath sounds on the right side. Matt knew what that meant: there was a tension pneumothorax, meaning that air was entering the space around the lungs but couldn't leave. The pressure from the air increased and caused the lung to collapse. If it wasn't treated fast, it could cause the mediastinum to be pushed to the other side, putting a kink in the main blood vessels and causing reduced cardiac output. Left longer, that meant a cardiac arrest and possibly death.

'I'm going to give you some oxygen,' Matt said, 'and I'm going to put a chest drain in to help you breathe better—it's going to hurt a bit, but hang on in there.' Deftly, he fitted the face mask, then pulled Patrick's shirt open and sprayed his skin around the area where he was going to make an incision. He grabbed a sixteen-gauge cannula, inserted it into the lower part of the second intercostal space, then withdrew the needle and listened for the hiss of air.

He exhaled sharply as he heard it. Good. He taped the cannula to the chest wall and inserted a chest drain. Patrick's colour was a bit better, but he still didn't seem to be breathing properly. Ah, hell. A tension pneumothorax was bad enough without complications.

He checked the oxygen saturations. Ninety-four. Not good enough.

Then he noticed that the bones in the outside wall of

Patrick's chest on the right-hand side were moving independently. Flail segment: so at least three ribs had broken in two places and could move independently. That meant when the patient breathed out, the flail segment moved in the opposite direction to the rest of the chest wall. In turn, that meant the patient's breathing wasn't fully effective—and so he was still in respiratory distress.

'Flail chest. Radio through to ED and alert ITU,' Matt said quietly to Dale. Flail chest often went with significant underlying injury to the lung, so Patrick would need to be treated in Intensive Care. Matt would guess that one of the broken ribs had punctured Patrick's lung. Plus bruising to the lung from where he'd landed on the fence meant that air wasn't being processed effectively. No wonder Patrick was still having problems breathing.

'Some of your ribs have broken in two places,' Matt explained to Patrick, 'and that's why it hurts so much. Does it hurt anywhere else?'

'No.'

'OK. We're going to put a collar on you to keep your neck still, just in case you might have a problem there, and I'm going to give you some morphine for the pain. Then we'll take you straight in to hospital. Can we ring your wife for you?'

'Can't. Train station. Picking up the in-laws,' Patrick gasped between rasping breaths.

'OK. We'll sort something out by the time we get to hospital,' Matt said.

Gently, he and Dale fitted the collar, lifted Patrick onto the trolley and headed straight for the emergency department.

Janice Horton came to meet them. 'What have you got?'

'Patrick, aged forty, fell off a ladder onto a fence and then to the driveway. Top to toe, he's got a cut on the head and a tension pneumothorax; I put a chest drain in at the scene, but he's still in respiratory distress even though the drain hasn't refilled. I've given him ten of morphine, sats ninety-four on oxygen, and it looks like flail segment to me, query punctured lung. We put a collar on to be on the safe side but he's not complaining of pain anywhere else, only his side.'

'Right. I'll sedate him and put him on a ventilator to get him more comfortable and get the air where I want it to be, then sort out a CT scan,' Janice said. 'Thanks, Matt. We've alerted ITU.'

'Cheers. We haven't been able to get in touch with his wife yet.' Matt handed her a sticky note. 'This is her number. She's picking her parents up from the train station.'

'OK, I'll get someone onto it.'

'Thanks. See you later,' Matt said.

He was about to leave the department when Shona came over to him. 'Hey, Matt. I wondered if you fancied breakfast in the canteen at the end of your shift? Or my place even?'

'Sorry,' he said, smiling at her to soften his words. 'It's really nice of you to offer, but I'm afraid I'm already meeting someone for breakfast.'

'Your girlfriend?' she guessed.

Right now, he couldn't answer that for sure. He hoped so, but until he'd seen Kelsey, talked to her, he just didn't know. 'Let's just say she's very special to me. I'm sorry.'

She shrugged. 'The nice ones are usually spoken for. I should've guessed.'

'We can still be friends.'

Oh, and how patronising that sounded.

And how bad he'd feel if Kelsey said those words to him tomorrow at breakfast.

He smiled awkwardly. 'Sorry. I didn't mean that to sound as bad as it did.'

She grinned. 'No worries. I'd already been warned you hardly ever date. She must be pretty special.'

'Yeah, she is.' He sighed. 'It's complicated.'

'I hope it works out for you.'

This time, his smile was genuine. 'Thanks. Catch you later.'

'That's it. I'm banning you from going anywhere near that coffee-machine,' Dale grumbled when another call came in.

'The Petrie flats.' Matt pulled a face. It was the most run-down estate in the city, and they all hated callouts to the area. A paramedic had been stabbed there the previous year for not giving up the drugs in the back of the ambulance. Alan, their station manager, had called them all in afterwards and told them that their lives just weren't worth risking. If any of the team got to the estate and the shout didn't seem quite right, they had to sit tight in the ambulance until there was police back-up. Which was hard, when all your instincts told you to go and save a life—but their safety had to come first. And half the calls from the Petrie flats were hoaxes anyway. 'My turn to drive,' Matt said. 'So what have we got?'

'Suspected heart attack,' Dale said.

'Don't tell me. Top floor of the flats?'

'Yep.'

Matt rolled his eyes. Most of the time the lifts didn't work so if it was a genuine call, he and Dale would probably have to carry their patient down a few flights of stairs. Stairs that usually stank of stale urine and vomit, and there were often contaminated sharps on window-sills and in corners. He just hoped their patient weighed less than a hundred kilos. Though if their patient was that heavy, he and Dale would need the fire crews there to help them do the lifting…

He shook himself. Yes, he wanted to see Kelsey. As soon as possible. But he didn't want her to have to face any danger in order to see him. And the Petrie flats were bad news.

Half the streetlights were out in the area round the Petrie flats. Cars were parked on both sides of the road, too, so it was a matter of picking your way through carefully and hoping that someone wasn't coming in the opposite direction.

Then Matt saw the headlights. Heading straight for them. At speed.

'Oh, come *on*,' he said, frustrated. Everyone knew if there was a blue light, you gave way. Let the emergency vehicle pass on its way to a shout.

But the other driver clearly didn't want to give way. Didn't want to pull in to the side and let the ambulance pass.

There wasn't room for two cars to pass in the middle of the road, let alone a car and an ambulance. But there was a gap just ahead on the left. If he could just make it…

But even as he swerved into the gap, he heard the crash of metal against metal. Felt the impact as the car ploughed into the ambulance. And everything went black.

CHAPTER THIRTEEN

'RTC BY THE Petrie flats. Car and an ambo, apparently,' Mark said, reading the fax transmission as he climbed into the back seat of the fire engine.

'An *ambulance*?' Kelsey went cold.

No. She was being paranoid. There were other ambulance crews in the region besides Matt's. But the Petrie flats were smack in the middle of his area…

As the fire engine roared off, she called Matt's mobile phone. Just in case.

'The mobile phone you are calling may be switched off,' the recorded message informed her.

OK. That didn't necessarily mean he'd been in the accident. He might already be on his way to the same shout. And when he was driving his phone was always switched off. She cut the call and punched in the number for the direct line to the crew at the ambulance station.

It was answered almost immediately: 'Kirk speaking.'

She bit back her dislike of Matt's colleague. 'Hi, it's Kelsey. Is Matt around?'

'He's on a shout.'

Unless it was her imagination running riot, Kirk sounded a bit jumpy. As part of the team, he'd know what was going on. 'Kirk, we've been called to a shout at the Petrie flats. Matt isn't involved, is he?'

'Um, can't talk right now. Shout coming in.'

'Kirk! Don't you d—'

Too late. He'd already hung up. She growled in frustration.

And the fact that he'd refused to answer her question meant it had to be Matt's ambulance.

'Brains? What's up?' Ray asked.

'That ambulance. I think it's Matt's.' She dragged in a breath. 'Kirk wouldn't deny it. And then he hung up on me. Said he had a shout.'

Ray made a pithy comment about Kirk—the rest of the crew shared Kelsey's less than complimentary view of the paramedic. 'If it *is* Matt's ambo, then you shouldn't be on this shout.'

'On the contrary.' Kelsey's voice was clipped. 'If it's Matt, I want to be there. I *need* to be there.'

Mark, who was sitting next to her, reached over to take her hand. 'Hey. It's a lot for anyone to cope with, seeing someone you care about in the middle of a smash-up.'

She pulled her hand away. 'And you think my head's already all over the place with this PTSD stuff, I'm not going to do my job properly?'

'He didn't say that, Brains,' Ray cut in. 'Lighten up. Look, we're your crew. Of course we're worried about you. I mean, if Lia was involved in an RTC and we were called out, you wouldn't want Mark to be there, would you? Or if we got to a shout and you recognised my wife's car, you'd tell me to keep back.'

'I suppose,' she admitted. 'But Matt isn't my husband.'

Mark rolled his eyes. 'He's as good as. Come on, Brains. We all know how you feel about him—and it's obvious how he feels about you. Isn't it time you admitted you two are more than just good friends?'

Maybe. But she wanted to tell Matt himself first. Tell him that she loved him.

'Guv, can you find out what the situation is?' she asked. 'Please?'

Ray radioed through to control. 'Vehicle 57. Any update about the Petrie flats incident?'

There was a pause, then the radio crackled. 'Police in attendance, two ambulances on their way to attend RTC and original call.'

'Any casualties?' Ray asked.

'Not sure. The ambulance is blocking the road, between a parked vehicle and the other vehicle involved in the collision.'

'Do we know who the crew is?' Kelsey asked urgently.

'Any identification of persons involved?' Ray asked.

'The information hasn't been released,' was the response.

'Thanks. Over and out.' He shifted round to look at Kelsey. 'Sorry, Brains,' he said with a sigh. 'We still don't know anything. But we're nearly there. We'll find out.' He looked levelly at her. 'And I want you to stay put until I can assess the situation.'

'If Matt's hurt, I need to be there,' she said stubbornly.

'You ought to be on sick leave,' Ray reminded her. 'I'm bending the rules for you as it is. If it's him, you stay out of it. Understood?'

Kelsey didn't reply. No way was she going to stand aside and do nothing if Matt was hurt.

'Kelsey!' This time Ray's voice was sharp.

'I promise I won't get in the way.' Which wasn't *quite* the same as promising to stay out of it, but Ray clearly wasn't in the mood to argue semantics because he didn't make her repeat his words.

They could see the blue flashing lights as they turned into the street. Two police cars and the smashed-up ambulance. But the second ambulance wasn't there yet.

'Stay put while I find out what's going on,' Ray told Kelsey sternly.

She could see enough for herself to know it wasn't good. The car had ploughed straight into the ambulance, smashing into the front on the driver's side at an angle. The impact had spun the ambulance into the parked cars on the left, and the car's bonnet was completely crumpled.

'We're going to need to cut them out,' Kelsey said to Joe.

'Leave it. The guv told you to stay put,' he reminded her. 'They'll do what's necessary.'

'If it's Matt…if he was driving…' Her throat felt thick, a mixture of nausea and choking tears.

'We don't know it's Matt.'

'His phone's on voicemail, and he only does that when he's driving. And Kirk wouldn't tell me that Matt was OK. So it *has* to be him, doesn't it?'

'Kirk's an idiot. He probably thought it'd be a laugh to wind you up. Matt's probably on another sh—' Joe stopped abruptly.

'It's him, isn't it?' Kelsey demanded, following Joe's gaze. Ray had already turned away, but she knew he'd made some kind of gesture to Joe.

'Brains? Where are you going?' Joe called.

Kelsey didn't answer. She was out of the fire engine and running.

Ray blocked her path before she got to the ambulance. 'Stay back.'

'No way.' She'd let Danny down. She'd let Mikey and Lucy down. So she definitely wasn't going to let Matt down. 'I'm the one with the ALS training. The other ambo isn't here yet, so you need my knowledge. You need me to help anyone who's hurt.' Meaning Matt. Not the driver who'd caused the crash.

'Kelsey, love—'

Oh, no. Oh, no, no, no. With that look on Ray's face—and the fact he'd used her real name rather than her nick-name—it wasn't good.

Please, God, don't let Matt be dead. Don't let him die before I can tell him I love him, Kelsey pleaded mentally. Don't let him die without knowing how much I care. Don't let him be badly hurt. Please. She dragged in a breath. 'Just tell me he's alive.'

Ray nodded. 'But he's unconscious.'

'Then he needs me. And I'm going to him. Throw the book at me for insubordination if you have to afterwards, but I'm going to him right now,' Kelsey said.

To her relief, he stepped aside. Out of her way.

She could see that Matt was hurt. Slumped in his seat. Unconscious. Just as Danny had been when the other car had smashed into them.

Oh, God, no. Please, don't let this be Danny all over again. Please, don't let her lose Matt the same way. He was proud, just as stubborn as Danny. If Matt didn't make a full recovery from his injuries, she knew he'd push her away, the same way Danny had done.

If he recovered at all.

'Matt?' she whispered through the smashed window. 'Matt, can you hear me? It's Kelsey.'

'Brains?' another voice croaked.

She recognised Dale's voice on the passenger's side

of the ambulance. She craned her neck to see. 'Hey, Dale. You OK?'

'Whiplash. And I'm going to have one hell of a seat-belt bruise.'

'Can you feel your hands, arms, legs and feet?' she asked. 'Can you move them?'

'I can feel them,' Dale said. 'But I can't move. I'm stuck under the dash.'

'Any pain I should know about?'

'Nah, I'll be OK. How's Matt?'

She swallowed. 'Unconscious.'

'Go through his vital signs,' Dale said. 'I can't move to do it myself. He's unconscious so we'll assume possible cervical spine injuries.'

'GCS,' Kelsey said, remembering her training. The Glasgow coma scale. 'Eyes first—Matt, can you open your eyes?' She dragged in a breath. 'No response. And he's not talking. He's not making a sound.'

'Won't be moving either, if he's unconscious. GCS three,' Dale said. 'KO's—I dunno how long. Since the smash. Go through the ABC next. Airway?'

She leaned in through the window. 'I think it's clear. Can't see any obstruction.' Not that she was in the best position to check. 'I can feel breath against my hand,' she said.

'Strong breathing?' Dale queried.

'Not very,' Kelsey admitted.

'You'll need to bag him maybe. Check his pulse.'

Kelsey did so—the point at his wrist was easiest to get to. She counted for fifteen seconds, checking against her watch. 'Bit fast. He's tachycardic.'

'OK. Can you reach the penlight torch in the pocket of his overalls?'

'Yes. Got it.'

'Check his eyes.'

She lifted the lids in turn and flashed the torch into them. 'Pupils equal and reactive,' Kelsey reported back.

'Good. Can you see any blood? Any cuts or bruises on his head?'

She gently stroked her fingertips across his scalp. No stickiness. 'Can't find any blood.'

'Good.' Dale sucked in a breath. 'Ah, my chest hurts.'

And his breathing sounded fast and shallow. Kelsey's heart missed a beat. 'Oh, no. Please, don't tell me you've got a tension pneumothorax. Not when I can't get to you to sort it.'

'I'll be fine.' Dale's breathing became more and more laboured as he spoke. 'Need to get a collar on Matt and bag him. When the ambo crew gets here, they'll intubate. Get fluids into him.'

Kelsey leaned backwards so she could call to Ray. 'Guv, I need access to the left side of the van so I can take a proper look at Dale. He's stuck under the dash. And I need to get in the back of the van, get the equipment out. Or ours if it's quicker.'

'The Hurst's on its way,' Ray told her. 'We'll get you access.'

'And where the hell's the ambo crew when you need them?' she asked.

'The police are clearing the area as much as they can,' Ray said. 'There are a couple more ambulances on their way.'

'Need more go-faster stripes,' Dale rasped.

'Stop talking,' Kelsey directed. 'And hang on in there. We're going to cut you out.'

'Wha' 'bou' Matt?'

Speaking was clearly becoming harder for Dale. 'Matt's going to be fine.' She wasn't at all sure about that, but the last thing she wanted was for Dale to panic. 'Hey, stop worrying. We're going to get both you out, I promise,' she said. 'And, Matt, you have to wake up. Help me here.' No response. Hell, hell, hell.

Or maybe there was another way. She knew what drove him: being needed. Fixing pain. Maybe if she told him how badly his skills were needed right now, it would penetrate his brain and somehow wake him up. 'Listen to me, Matt Fraser. I'm a firefighter, not a paramedic! I've been on a course but I don't know everything *you* know. Wake *up*. I need you to talk me through what I have to do.'

Still no response.

'I'll do it. Get collar. From back,' Dale wheezed. 'And mask. Oxygen.'

She knew what he was getting at. Something Matt had once told her. If the casualty wasn't getting enough oxygen, they'd die anyway no matter what you did. Hypoxia. And Matt wasn't breathing well enough on his own. He needed help.

But the back doors were stuck.

Mark was already hefting an axe and she could see gashes in the back where he was working on releasing the door. She grabbed another one from the equipment stash. 'Alternate strokes. You, me, you, me,' she said.

The axes smashed into the van over and over again, and Kelsey threw all her strength behind every stroke. She'd get Matt out of there. She would. She'd get him out and make him safe.

Kelsey had just dragged the rear doors of the ambulance open when she heard a siren wailing and another ambulance pulled up. Her grip on the axe tightened when she saw Kirk climb out, but she forced herself to relax and hand it back to Mark.

'What's happened?' Kirk asked as he ran over to them.

'Dale's got a tension pneumothorax. Matt's unconscious, breathing not good, GCS three and his pupils are
equal and reactive. We can't get either of them out until
we've cut through.'

'I'll go in through the back, now you've opened it,' Kirk
said. 'Dale first because it's a quick fix.' And because a
tension pneumothorax was life-threatening. 'Alec's dealing
with the other vehicle. I'll need you to assist me.'

Good. Because if Kirk had even suggested she couldn't
be with Matt, she'd have scalped him. Besides, she was
going to be needed in there to hold the shield over Dale and
Matt while the fire crews cut them out.

Kirk climbed into the ambulance; she took the tear
shield from Mark and followed Kirk.

Kirk quickly assessed both his colleagues, and put an
oxygen mask on Matt. 'I need to put a drain in Dale's
chest,' he told Kelsey. 'Can you pass me a cannula?'

She could hardly hear him, with the noise from the
cutting gear. 'What gauge?' she yelled back.

'Sixteen. Fast as you can.'

Kelsey rummaged in the bag and handed him the cannula.

'Spray,' Kirk directed.

She passed that to him, too, and held the tear sheet to
protect Dale from any debris. Meanwhile Kirk sprayed
the area before he put the cannula into the second intercostal space.

'I can't hear. Tell them to stop for a minute,' Kirk yelled.
'I need to hear the air.'

If he hadn't punctured the air bubble, the pressure on
Dale's chest would get worse and there was a chance he'd
have a heart attack.

And all the time Matt was still unconscious, Kelsey

thought as she climbed out of the ambulance and joined the fire crew again. Supposing she'd missed something? Supposing he had a subarachnoid haemorrhage? Supposing he was dying right now?

'Stop the cutting,' she yelled to Ray. 'Not long, just thirty seconds. Kirk needs to hear if he's sorted Dale.'

The noise of the cutters stopped, and the silence felt weirdly loud.

Come *on*, Kirk, she thought desperately. How much longer was he going to be? They needed to cut Matt out of the ambulance and get him to the emergency department. The longer it took, the more likely it was that he'd deteriorate. They'd already used up way too much of the golden hour for her liking.

When she heard him yell, 'Got it!' she realised that she'd been holding her breath. She exhaled sharply. 'OK. I'm coming back in.'

'Tubing,' Kirk yelled as the cutters started up again.

She handed him the tubing.

'And can you hold Matt's head in neutral while I finish sorting this out?' Kirk added.

'OK.' She left the tear shield in place and knelt behind Matt, supporting his head and neck while Kirk put the drain in Dale's chest.

'Wake up,' she said to Matt. 'Please, wake up. I can't lose you like this.'

No response. Not that she'd expected any. He was still out cold.

'I love you.' She didn't care that Kirk the jerk and Dale were right next to her. They wouldn't be able to hear anyway through the noise of the cutters. But Matt might be able to hear her. He'd know her touch. Maybe her voice would help pull him through this. 'I love you and

I'm going to get you out of here. Everything's going to be all right.'

Five years ago, it hadn't been. She'd been trapped in a vehicle and had needed to be cut out. And the driver—Danny—had been unconscious. For a moment the past and the present blurred. She remembered the fear. How she'd been sure that Danny was dead and neither of them would make it out of the crushed car. How she'd held his unresponsive fingers in hers and begged him to wake up. The metallic smell of blood all around her. The noise of the cutters, the feel of the vibrations in her head. The blinding light in her eyes as the crew had worked. The taste of blood in her mouth.

It was all happening again.

Except she'd done this countless times since then. Sat in the back and held the driver's neck in neutral while the fire crew wielded cutters and released the occupants. She wasn't at risk in the slightest. She was trained to deal with this.

'I should have told you before,' she said fiercely to Matt. 'I love you. I've loved you for a long, long time—except I kidded myself you were just my best mate. But you're the one I look for first thing in the morning. You're the one I come home to after the day from hell. You're the one who's going to open the champagne when I make crew manager—and we'll go dancing till dawn.' She dragged in a breath. 'You're the one I want to be with, through the good times and the bad. Only you. So you have to wake up, Matt. You have to wake up so I can tell you properly.'

But there was no response.

Again, the past and the present blurred. She'd done this before, in the days when Danny had been either unconscious or sedated, while his broken body had settled down enough for the surgeons to assess the situation and work out the best way of treating him. She'd sat holding his hand, talking to him. Talking about everything and nothing. Willing him to pull through.

He had.

And then he'd rejected her.

But that had been then. This was now. Different man. Different feelings.

'Don't you give up on me,' she told Matt shakily. 'Don't you *dare* give up on me. Because I sure as hell won't give up on you. Whatever happens, I'm staying with you. And everything's going to be all right.'

And maybe, if she said it often enough, it would come true. 'Everything's going to be fine. I love you.'

Just at that moment, the cutters stopped. And her words echoed through the van.

I love you.

'You picked your time to tell him,' Kirk said.

'It's nothing to do with you,' she flashed back. 'So just keep out of it, will you?'

'Ow,' Dale said loudly. 'That chest drain hurts. And your bedside manner leaves a lot to be desired.'

'Did the job, didn't I? You can breathe again.' Kirk handed Dale an oxygen mask. 'Stick this on. But before you do, what the hell happened?'

'We had a shout to a heart attack. Except we never got there. This guy was steaming along towards us. Matt tried to avoid him…' Dale grimaced and put the mask against his nose and mouth, sucking in oxygen for a moment, then lifted the mask off again. 'Didn't have time to get in the space.'

'Keep holding him, Kelsey. I'm going to put the collar on Dale so your lot can lift him out.'

'We still need to do a dash roll,' Kelsey warned. 'He's stuck. The front of the van's been pushed in. Matt's legs might be trapped, too.'

'Any chest injuries?'

'I'd only just started to check him when you arrived,' Kelsey said.

'Better assume he smacked into the steering-wheel. Query fractured sternum.' Kirk finished fitting the hard collar, directed the fire crew to get Dale out and put him in the back of the ambulance, then turned to Matt. 'I'm going to take the mask off, intubate him properly and put two large cannulae in his forearm. We might need to get fluids into him quickly,' he said to Kelsey. 'And I want to know why he's still out.'

'Must have hit his head. But I couldn't find a wound, and his pupils were OK,' Kelsey said.

'We need him in for a CT scan and chest X-rays. And I want him on oxygen all the way from here to Resus.' Kirk finished fitting the collar, then did the intubation and cannulae. 'Help me get the spinal board on him.'

She did so in silence. Again, it was something she'd done countless times before. But this time it was different. This time the board was going on the person who meant most to her in the whole world.

'Kirk. Is he going to pull through?' she whispered.

'Let's get him out of here. They'll know more in Resus.'

He didn't answer the question, she noted. And her misery must have shown because, just for a moment, he squeezed her arm. 'Me and Matt, we don't get along that well. But he's a bloody good paramedic. He's one of the team. I'll do my best for him.'

'Yeah.' She could barely push the word out past the lump in her throat. 'Can I…?'

'Go with him in the back? Yeah. If your guv agrees.'

Ray agreed straight away, enveloping her in a bear hug. 'Call us when you can. Anything you need, you've got it.

And don't worry about coming in for your shift. We'll cover you as long as we need to.'

'Thanks, guv.'

She climbed into the back of the ambulance with Matt, and the doors slammed shut behind her. Seeing Matt with a nasogastric tube in place and the mask and the hard collar taped to him shocked her. Even though she'd seen the procedure countless times before, this time it was personal. She couldn't see much of his face. Couldn't kiss him or hold him in her arms. All she could do was hold his hand and will him to hang on in there.

Just like she'd done with Danny—except he'd been cut out first and had already been on his way to hospital before she'd been freed from their car.

This time it was different. She was fine. She hadn't been involved in the accident. And she'd stay with Matt. Be the first one he saw when he woke up.

She just had to pray it was a when, not an if.

The next few hours were a blur. Kelsey went with Matt's stretcher to Resus, waited in Radiology while he had a CT scan, and then sat outside Theatre while they removed the clot the scan had revealed in his brain. She had no idea how long it took or even what the time was—time had stopped having any meaning in the window-less area outside Theatre. She was bone-weary, but she couldn't sleep. Couldn't rest. Not until she knew Matt was going to be all right.

Just as she'd sat at Danny's bedside, she sat by Matt's in Intensive Care, dozing in the chair next to him and only leaving the room for long enough to have a quick shower and put on the change of clothes that Mark's wife Lia had brought her, or when the nurses pushed her out and made her go to the canteen for something to eat. She had no idea what she ate or drank. The only thing she could focus on was Matt.

Please, please, let him pull through this.

'Any news?' Ray asked when he called at the hospital to see her.

She shook her head. 'They're keeping him sedated until the swelling in his brain goes down.' She knew she sounded cool, calm and collected. She had to. Because if she didn't keep her emotions firmly battened down, she'd be crying. Sobbing. And she didn't know if she would ever stop. So it was better not to start.

'Hey. He'll pull through. He's made of tough stuff.' Ray gave her a hug.

She wanted to cling to him and howl, but she couldn't let herself. Instead, she stayed absolutely still. Like a fragile piece of glass that could be snapped by too much handling.

'Anything you need? Anything you want one of us to bring for you from home?'

All she wanted was for him to go away. Leave her with Matt. Let her concentrate on the man she loved and will him back to a full recovery. 'No, I'm fine, thanks.'

'You look like hell,' Ray said, shaking his head. 'Are you sure you should be here?'

'Better here than at home. It's the waiting. It's—' She clamped her lips together and wrapped her arms round herself. She wasn't going to break down. Not here, not now, not ever. She'd be strong for Matt. 'I just want him to wake up,' she whispered.

'He will.' Ray gave her another hug. 'Hey. You just call me if you need anything. Me or one of the guys. We'll be here.'

She nodded. 'Thanks.'

And then she was back at Matt's bedside. On her own.

Tubes and wires everywhere. 'You're going to get through this,' she told him softly, rubbing her thumb against the back of his hand. '*We're* going to get through this. Together.'

Dale was her next visitor.

'Don't hug me,' he warned. 'I hurt like hell. Kirk's a butcher.'

'At least he got it in first time. If you'd had to talk me through it, you'd have a few more holes in you.'

He grinned. 'Nah. We'd still have you on our team any time you want to swap a red motor for a white one. And you can be an honorary paramedic on our quiz team in the pub.' His grin faded. 'So how's he doing?'

'Still sedated. And he's got a cracked sternum as well.'

'Ouch.' Dale winced. 'If it's any consolation, the occupants of the other car have a few broken bones. And they'll be healing in prison.'

'Prison?' What was he on about?

'Armed robbers. Apparently, they'd just held up the off-licence by the Petrie flats.' He pulled a face. 'That's why they weren't so keen to give way when they saw us coming. They thought the police wouldn't be that far behind.'

Kelsey dragged in a breath. 'So they just smacked into you.'

'Probably thought they could force us off the road and get past. Been watching too many bad crime dramas on telly,' Dale said dryly. 'And you look terrible. Have you had any sleep at all?'

'I'm not leaving Matt.'

'You need to look after yourself,' he warned. 'You're not going to be able to help him if you collapse.'

'I won't collapse.' She bit her lip. 'Been here before, haven't I? I know the drill.'

Dale winced. 'Sorry. Put my size twelves in it. Look,

I'll sit with Matt for a while and you can have a break. Go and have a cup of tea or something.'

'I don't want tea.' She just wanted Matt.

'Go for a walk and get some fresh air, then,' Dale said. 'He's not going anywhere.'

'And neither am I,' Kelsey insisted.

She dragged through two more days of the same. And then she came back from a shower one morning and stopped dead.

Matt's eyes were open.

Those beautiful cornflower-blue eyes that made her melt.

'Matt?' she whispered.

'Hey.' His voice sounded cracked. 'Nurse tells me I got a fiancée.'

She flushed as she sat down beside his bed. Hell. She'd presumed too much. 'Well, it was the only way they'd let me stay. If they thought I was…more than a friend.'

'Yeah?' A corner of his mouth quirked. 'So are you?'

She wanted to be. But this wasn't the right time to discuss it. 'You've had major surgery. You're in Intensive Care. You're supposed to be resting.' She took a shuddering breath. 'And you *would* wait for the second I left your bedside to wake up, wouldn't you?'

'Been there long?'

'Dunno. Don't ask me what day it is. But no way was I leaving here.' She sat very, very still. 'You scared me, Matt. I thought I'd lost you.' She swallowed hard. 'Lost you before I could tell you.'

'Tell me what?'

'Something I should've told you a long time ago.' She folded her hand round his. 'That I love you. That you mean the world to me.'

'What 'bout Danny?'

'Sorted. I told you.' Her eyes widened. 'Can't you remember talking to me about it?'

'No. Crash. Sorry,' he mumbled.

'Hey. Don't be sorry. It wasn't your fault. But next time you see some armed robbers driving straight for you, get out of the way, eh?'

His eyes crinkled at the corners. 'Yeah. So tired, Kels.'

'Rest. Just rest. I'm not going anywhere. I'll be here when you wake up again.'

'Good. Love you, Kels.'

As his eyes closed, a tear slid down her cheek. He loved her. And now he knew she loved him. She just had to hope he'd pull through this. That they could make their new start.

'You all right, love?' the nurse asked as she came in to do Matt's neurological observations.

'I think so. He's asleep again but he came to for a while.'

The nurse nodded. 'Yes, when you were in the shower. I told him you hadn't gone far. He's going to be up and down for a while. And also he's going to be very, very tired.'

'But I can stay?' Kelsey pleaded.

'As long as you let him rest. No excitement.'

She smiled wryly. 'Considering we're both in the emergency services… No. I won't let him get agitated. Promise.' She just wanted to take care of him. Heal his hurt. Put him first.

The next time Matt came to, Kelsey was holding his hand.

'Hey, sleepy.' She stroked his face. 'How're you doing?'

'Ache in bits I didn't know I had.' He grimaced. 'Did I dream you here?'

'When?'

'Don't know. You said…' He stopped, looking unsure.

'I said I loved you. And I do. But you're supposed to be resting—we'll have this conversation later.'

'You have to marry me now.' He smiled. 'You allowed everyone to believe you're my fiancée.'

She grinned. 'If that's meant to be a proposal, Matt Fraser… No, you can wait till you're better. I want a proper proposal. Down on one knee.'

His smile faded. 'What if…?'

He didn't need to ask the question. The fear was all over his face.

'You'll pull through. The doctor reckons you're going to make a full recovery. It'll take a bit of time, but you'll be fine. You're not going to be in a wheelchair and there won't be any permanent damage from the brain clot.' She paused. 'And even if you didn't make a full recovery, you wouldn't get rid of me so easily.'

He flinched. 'I don't want you to stay out of pity.'

Danny, all over again. Well, this time she wasn't going to let it happen. 'I'm not staying out of pity. I'm here because I love you. Because I want to be with you. Because without you the sun would stop shining. Now, stop fretting and get some rest, will you? Otherwise they'll chuck me out for letting you get agitated and I'll go crazy if I can't be with you.'

'Uh-huh.' His hand tightened round hers. 'Love you. Always.'

'Me, too. And I'm sorry it's taken me so long to tell you.'

''Sall right. Told me now. That's what matters.' He tried to smile. 'Can't keep my eyes open.'

'It's OK. I'm staying put. Got a stack of notes to work through while you're asleep.'

'Studying?'

'Yeah. Though I'll have to take a rain-check on my back-rub.'

He chuckled. 'Want to do more than a backrub.'

She grinned. 'Not in Intensive Care. They'll skin me.'

'When I get home?'

'We can't *have* this conversation, Matt. If your pulse or your blood pressure goes up, one of those machines is going to beep and I'll be in trouble.'

'You're a firefighter. Live dangerously.'

She laughed. 'Yeah. When we get home.'

And, hour by hour, she was beginning to hope that this was going to work out. That Matt was going to pull through. And they were going to get their happy ever after.

CHAPTER FOURTEEN

Two months later, Matt was sitting at the kitchen table with a bad case of the fidgets. 'It's a perfect autumn day. The sun is shining, the leaves are crisp underfoot, there's that lovely smoky smell in the air—'

'And you're supposed to be taking it easy,' Kelsey reminded him. 'You're recovering from having a clot removed from inside your head, not to mention a cracked sternum and the most horrendous bruising. You're absolutely not fit to go back to work yet.'

'Who said anything about work? It's your day off. Wouldn't you like to go to Dovedale for a teensy little stroll?' he wheedled.

She knew exactly what he had in mind. One of their afternoon tramps through the Dales. She could manage it, but she knew he couldn't yet. 'No chance. You're not up to a four-hour hike.'

'We don't have to do a proper walk. Well, not much further than the car park. Look, if we go to the car park near the stepping stones, I can walk to the river and back again. I could just do with a change of scenery and a bit of fresh air. And gentle exercise is good for me. My consultant said so,' he added, narrowing his eyes.

Oh, so he was bringing in the big guns now? Kelsey folded her arms. 'On one condition. If you're tired, you admit it straight away and we go straight back to the car. I don't want you overdoing it and setting yourself back.'

He grinned. 'Have I told you lately how bossy you are?'

She grinned back. 'You don't need to. I already know. So do you agree to the condition?'

'Give me a kiss and it's a deal.' He pushed his chair back and patted his lap.

Kelsey smiled and sat on his lap. She brushed the hair back from his forehead and slid her arms round his neck. 'I can't believe how well you're recovering. In that ambulance, I was so scared I'd lose you,' she said, rubbing her nose against his.

'No way. I'd have come back, like the bloke in that weepy film you love. You know, the one with the cello.'

Truly, Madly, Deeply.

'Which is how I love you.' He kissed her lightly. 'I've loved you for ages. Since…I dunno. There's always been that spark between us. But I told myself I didn't want to get involved with anyone after Cassie, and you always made it clear you were married to the fire brigade.'

'I was. But then there was you. All the little things— they added up and I realised I'd grown to depend on you. The way you cook for me. The way you stop me overdoing it when I'm studying. Your massages.'

He grinned. 'You're not doing so badly yourself in the massage department, Miss Watson. Except you're too easily distracted.'

'Mmm.' She wriggled on his lap. 'And whose fault is that? Rolling over just when I start to move your towel down…'

'Doesn't mean you *have* to touch me.' He grinned. 'But I kind of like it that you can't keep your hands off me.'

She laughed. 'I was inspecting your bruises. Seeing how well they're healing.'

'Were you, hell. I didn't have any bruising anywhere *near* the area you were inspecting.' He tightened his arms round her waist. 'I don't know when I fell in love with you. But I know exactly when I realised I wanted you to be with me for the rest of your life.' He traced her jawline with his mouth. 'The moment Mark brought you out of that fire and pushed you through the window into my arms. I'd been going crazy, knowing you were in there and not knowing if you were all right. That's when I realised you're the centre of my life.'

'It was about the same time for me. That night when you held me, pushed the nightmares away… I woke up in the morning and I knew I wanted it to happen every morning. Waking in your arms. But I didn't think you wanted to get involved. Not after Cassie.'

'I didn't. But you got under my skin. I found I liked being around you. Not to mention the fact that I wanted you. Badly.' He smiled. 'Do you have any idea how tough it was for me to give you that back massage and not just carry you upstairs to my bed?'

'Don't even think about it,' she warned, seeing the gleam in his eyes. 'You're not up to carrying me. Not until you've healed properly.'

'Spoilsport.' He kissed her lightly. 'I can't believe that when you finally said you loved me, you did it in front of the fire crew—and Kirk, of all people.'

'Kirk's not so bad. He stabilised you after the crash.'

'He says you were holding an axe.'

'I had to get the back of the van open.' She rubbed her nose against his. 'But I was pretty wound up. Worried sick about you. If he'd said I had to stay out of the way, I might've threatened him with it.' She rolled her eyes. 'He actually had the cheek to say my timing was off. But it wasn't supposed to be like that. Nobody else was supposed to hear. The cutting gear stopped when I wasn't expecting it to.'

'And you were yelling at the top of your voice that you loved me.' He grinned. 'Anyone ever explain to you that you're supposed to tell the one you love before you tell other people?'

'I'd planned to. Over breakfast on Friday morning. Except you had an argument with a car and scuppered all my plans.' She brushed her mouth over his. 'You gave me a bad scare, Matt.'

'Says the woman who goes to fight fires without enough oxygen in her tank. You've done your fair share of scaring,' he reminded her.

'Calculated risks.'

'Hmm. We'll have to agree to disagree,' he said. 'I still can't quite get over you telling the nursing staff that you were my fiancée. I thought I was hallucinating when that nurse told me that my wife-to-be hadn't left my side for more than about three minutes. I had no idea what she was talking about. I didn't even have an official girlfriend, let alone a fiancée. And then you walked in, with your hair still wet from the shower.' He smiled. 'You looked like an angel.'

'Angel?' She laid her hand against his forehead. 'Hmm, no sign of a temperature.'

'Oh, ha, ha.' His smile faded. 'And then I was worried in case you were only there out of guilt.'

'No. I was there because I wanted to be with you,' she said simply. 'Because I realised how much you mattered to me. Without you, nothing mattered any more. Not my job, not my life here—and this house would've been way too empty without you.'

'Let's go to Dovedale,' Matt said. 'I just want to walk hand in hand with you by the river.'

'Going soppy since that brain operation?' she teased.

'Something like that.'

She grinned, and kissed him. 'OK. But I mean it. No overdoing things. No heroics. One small walk.'

'Promise.'

She drove them out into the Dales and parked where he directed.

'Remember last time we came here?' Matt asked as they walked towards the river. 'I was trying to get you to admit you had PTSD.'

'I've admitted it now,' Kelsey said. 'And I'm doing something about it. The therapy's going well.'

'I noticed you managed to drive past the school on the way here,' Matt said. 'That's a good sign.'

'Yeah.' She bit her lip. 'I still feel bad about it, but I realise now that it wasn't my fault. Nobody else would have been able to get those kids out either. It was just bad luck, a combination of things that nobody could have predicted.'

'Good.' Matt tightened his fingers round hers. 'And the flashbacks have stopped.'

'Pretty much.'

'And you don't feel bad about Danny any more.'

'No. He's happy. He's made a new life for himself, one that doesn't include me except as a friend.'

'So we're both on the road to recovery.'

'There's a way to go yet—but, yes, you're right.' She smiled at him. 'And the future's looking good.'

'You think so?'

'Yeah. You and me—we're OK. We make a great team. I kind of like the way we are now. Still best friends—but lovers, too.' Since Matt had come home, they'd shared the same bedroom. And Kelsey loved waking in Matt's arms every morning. The feel of his body curved round hers made her feel warm and safe and protected, not stifled.

'Hmm,' Matt said.

Kelsey frowned. 'What?'

'Let's just stop here a minute.'

Something in his tone alerted her. 'Matt? Do you need to sit down?'

'No.' He dropped to one knee. 'Something else. Something you said to me in hospital.'

She stared at him, eyes wide. 'What?'

'You said you wanted a proper proposal. Down on one knee. So here I am.' He took her left hand and kissed her ring finger. 'Kelsey Watson, will you please do me the honour of marrying me?'

She blinked. 'You want to marry me?'

'Yes. I've been planning this for weeks. I went out last week to get you a ring—when I told you Dale was taking me out for coffee.'

'That's *sneaky*.'

He smiled. 'Worked, though. Kels, I don't care if it's the two of us getting married in a tiny little register office, or a huge wedding with the entire fire and ambulance service there as a guard of honour with fire axes and splints. Just as long as you make that promise in front of witnesses. For richer, for poorer. Better or worse. My lawful wedded wife. My love, my equal partner.'

'For as long as we both shall live?' She smiled. 'Yeah, I think I can take those vows. Not the obedience one,' she added with a grin, 'but I agree to the rest of them.'

He grinned back. 'I didn't expect obedience. Not from you. But love and honour will do very nicely.'

'Not to mention worshipping you with my body,' she suggested.

His grin broadened. 'Oh, yes. You can do that as much as you like. Except I think we should go home first. If we do the body-worshipping bit in the middle of Dovedale, we might get arrested.'

Her eyes glittered. 'I'll make one promise now.' She leaned down and kissed him. 'I love you, Matt Fraser. I love you with every single cell in my body. And I'll love and honour you for the rest of my days.'

He kissed her back. 'Me, too. I love you, Kelsey Watson. I want to grow old with you. Live with you and love with you and laugh with you.' He held her gaze. 'For the rest of my days.'

And that was when Kelsey knew for sure. Everything was going to be just fine.

MILLS & BOON®

Live the emotion

Medical
romance™

CARING FOR HIS CHILD by *Amy Andrews*

On arrival at Ashworth Bay, Fran Holloway meets her handsome neighbour, Dr David Ross, and his young daughter Mirry. Fran longs to be close to them, but her feelings after losing her own daughter are still raw. Fran finds herself falling for David, but can she risk her heart once again?

THE SURGEON'S SPECIAL GIFT
by *Fiona McArthur*

Bachelor Dads – Single Doctors…Single Fathers!

Dr Ailee Green knows she *cannot* start a relationship with Dr Fergus McVicker. Yet when she sees the handsome single father and his daughter, Ailee knows she can give them one gift before she goes – she can help them be the family they deserve. However, when Fergus offers his unconditional love, her determination begins to waver!

A DOCTOR BEYOND COMPARE
by *Melanie Milburne*

Top-Notch Docs
He's not just the boss, he's the best there is!

Recently single, Dr Holly Saxby has to leave the city ASAP. So she packs up her designer clothes and heads to Baronga Bay. She's not quite ready for the beach life, and she certainly isn't expecting ruggedly handsome Dr Cameron McCarrick to be her new partner…

On sale 1st September 2006

Available at WHSmith, Tesco, ASDA, Borders, Eason, Sainsbury's and most bookshops

www.millsandboon.co.uk

MILLS & BOON®

Live the emotion

0806/03b

_Medical
romance™

RESCUED BY MARRIAGE by *Dianne Drake*

Dr Della Riordan is in need of some luck – she really needs to get her life back on track! The practice on Redcliffe Island seems too good to be true; with gorgeous Dr Sam Montgomery on hand to help, Della begins to find her feet… But Sam is hiding a secret that could well bring an end to Della's dreams.

THE NURSE'S LONGED-FOR FAMILY
by *Fiona Lowe*

Jess Henderson is balancing her nursing job with being mother to Woody, her two-year-old nephew. Gorgeous Dr Alex Fitzwilliam manages to convince her that there is always time for romance… But Alex refuses to confront his feelings over the loss of his own son. Alex must put his feelings aside if they have any chance of becoming a family.

HER BABY'S SECRET FATHER
by *Lynne Marshall*

When Nurse Jaynie Winchester goes into premature labour, no-one comes rushing to her side. Baby Tara is delivered, and Jaynie is not the only one willing the tiny mite to survive. Respiratory therapist Terrance Zanderson finds himself getting involved with this family, then Terrance realises who Tara's father is…

On sale 1st September 2006

Available at WHSmith, Tesco, ASDA, Borders, Eason, Sainsbury's and most bookshops

www.millsandboon.co.uk

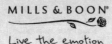

MILLS & BOON®

Live the emotion

Heart of a Hero

Featuring
The Paramedic's Secret by Lilian Darcy
Police Doctor by Laura MacDonald
Fire Rescue by Abigail Gordon

Make sure you buy these irresistible stories!

On sale 1st September 2006

Available at WHSmith, Tesco, ASDA, Borders, Eason, Sainsbury's and most bookshops

www.millsandboon.co.uk

"I was fifteen when my mother finally told me the truth about my father. She didn't mean to. She meant to keep it a secret forever. If she'd succeeded it might have saved us all."

When a hauntingly familiar stranger knocks on Roberta Dutreau's door, she is compelled to begin a journey of self-discovery leading back to her childhood. But is she ready to know the truth about what happened to her, her best friend Cynthia and their mothers that tragic night ten years ago?

16th June 2006

MIRA®

FREE

4 BOOKS AND A SURPRISE GIFT!

We would like to take this opportunity to thank you for reading this Mills & Boon® book by offering you the chance to take FOUR more specially selected titles from the Medical Romance™ series absolutely FREE! We're also making this offer to introduce you to the benefits of the Mills & Boon® Reader Service™—

- ★ **FREE home delivery**
- ★ **FREE gifts and competitions**
- ★ **FREE monthly Newsletter**
- ★ **Books available before they're in the shops**
- ★ **Exclusive Reader Service offers**

Accepting these FREE books and gift places you under no obligation to buy; you may cancel at any time, even after receiving your free shipment. Simply complete your details below and return the entire page to the address below. You don't even need a stamp!

YES! Please send me 4 free Medical Romance books and a surprise gift. I understand that unless you hear from me, I will receive 6 superb new titles every month for just £2.80 each, postage and packing free. I am under no obligation to purchase any books and may cancel my subscription at any time. The free books and gift will be mine to keep in any case.

M6ZEE

Ms/Mrs/Miss/Mr.............................Initials ....
                                                                  BLOCK CAPITALS PLEASE

Surname ....

Address ....

....

....Postcode ....

Send this whole page to:
The Reader Service, FREEPOST CN81, Croydon, CR9 3WZ